A CASTLE OF DREAMS

The Duke strode across the hall and then stopped as a sudden flash of pale blue caught his eye.

The most beautiful girl he had ever seen in his life was gliding down the great stairway towards him.

He did not see the costly dress or even the sparkling sapphires at her neck.

All he could see was the sheer beauty of her face, the proud way she held her head, the tumbled golden curls, carelessly pinned back with a length of cream lace.

He had not the faintest idea who she was or who could introduce him.

Normally the Duke was a quiet reserved man, but some power held him in place at the foot of the stairs and as the angel in blue reached him, he held out his hand and asked her gently,

"Madam, please will you do the honour of dancing with me?"

Viola felt as if she had been swept away into an unknown world.

D1549359

THE BARBARA CARTLAND PINK COLLECTION

Titles in this series

A CASTLE OF DREAMS

BARBARA CARTLAND

Barbaracartland.com Ltd

Copyright © 2009 by Cartland Promotions
First published on the internet in August 2009
by Barbaracartland.com

ISBN 978-1-906950-07-1

*The characters and situations in this book are entirely
imaginary and bear no relation to any real person or
actual happening.*

This book is sold subject to the condition that it shall not,
by way of trade or otherwise, be lent, resold, hired out or
otherwise circulated without the publisher's prior consent.

No part of this publication may be reproduced or
transmitted in any form or by any means, electronically or
mechanically, including photocopying, recording or any
information storage or retrieval, without the prior
permission in writing from the publisher.

Printed and bound in Great Britain by Cle-Print Ltd.
of St Ives, Cambridgeshire.

THE BARBARA CARTLAND PINK COLLECTION

Barbara Cartland was the most prolific bestselling author in the history of the world. She was frequently in the Guinness Book of Records for writing more books in a year than any other living author. In fact her most amazing literary feat was when her publishers asked for more Barbara Cartland romances, she doubled her output from 10 books a year to over 20 books a year, when she was 77.

She went on writing continuously at this rate for 20 years and wrote her last book at the age of 97, thus completing 400 books between the ages of 77 and 97.

Her publishers finally could not keep up with this phenomenal output, so at her death she left 160 unpublished manuscripts, something again that no other author has ever achieved.

Now the exciting news is that these 160 original unpublished Barbara Cartland books are already being published and by Barbaracartland.com exclusively on the internet, as the international web is the best possible way of reaching so many Barbara Cartland readers around the world.

The 160 books are published monthly and will be numbered in sequence.

The series is called the Pink Collection as a tribute to Barbara Cartland whose favourite colour was pink and it became very much her trademark over the years.

The Barbara Cartland Pink Collection is published only on the internet. Log on to www.barbaracartland.com to find out how you can purchase the books monthly as they are published, and take out a subscription that will ensure that all subsequent editions are delivered to you by mail order to your home.

NEW

Barbaracartland.com is proud to announce the publication of ten new Audio Books for the first time as CDs. They are favourite Barbara Cartland stories read by well-known actors and actresses and each story extends to 4 or 5 CDs. The Audio Books are as follows:

The Patient Bridegroom	The Passion and the Flower
A Challenge of Hearts	Little White Doves of Love
A Train to Love	The Prince and the Pekinese
The Unbroken Dream	A King in Love
The Cruel Count	A Sign of Love

More Audio Books will be published in the future and the above titles can be purchased by logging on to the website www.barbaracartland.com or please write to the address below.

If you do not have access to a computer, you can write for information about the Barbara Cartland Pink Collection and the Barbara Cartland Audio Books to the following address:

Barbara Cartland.com Ltd., Camfield Place,
Hatfield, Hertfordshire AL9 6JE, United Kingdom.
Telephone: +44 (0)1707 642629
Fax: +44 (0)1707 663041

THE LATE DAME BARBARA CARTLAND

Barbara Cartland who sadly died in May 2000 at the age of nearly 99 was the world's most famous romantic novelist who wrote 723 books in her lifetime with worldwide sales of over 1 billion copies and her books were translated into 36 different languages.

As well as romantic novels, she wrote historical biographies, 6 autobiographies, theatrical plays, books of advice on life, love, vitamins and cookery. She also found time to be a political speaker and television and radio personality.

She wrote her first book at the age of 21 and this was called *Jigsaw*. It became an immediate bestseller and sold 100,000 copies in hardback and was translated into 6 different languages. She wrote continuously throughout her life, writing bestsellers for an astonishing 76 years. Her books have always been immensely popular in the United States, where in 1976 her current books were at numbers 1 & 2 in the B. Dalton bestsellers list, a feat never achieved before or since by any author.

Barbara Cartland became a legend in her own lifetime and will be best remembered for her wonderful romantic novels, so loved by her millions of readers throughout the world.

Her books will always be treasured for their moral message, her pure and innocent heroines, her good looking and dashing heroes and above all her belief that the power of

"We all dream about romantic castles rising out of the mist in a beautiful setting. For me Scotland with all its turbulent history and wonderful heritage has to be the most romantic country in the world."

Barbara Cartland

CHAPTER ONE
1904

Lady Viola Northcombe stared at her reflection in the old misted cheval mirror that stood in the corner of her bedroom and sighed.

She was supremely unaware of the beauty of her face, surrounded as it was by tumbling blonde curls, her eyes the most startling violet blue fringed with dark lashes that swept down onto pink cheeks.

No, all Lady Viola could see at the moment was the old-fashioned, ivory lace ball gown she was wearing.

At nineteen Viola was not a fashion conscious girl.

She was more than happy wearing riding clothes or a plain cotton dress to sit in the garden.

But tonight was a special occasion and she wished she looked just a little more – well, special!

"Nanny, is there anything we can do to make this look a little more fashionable, a little more up to date?" she asked as a round-faced, elderly woman dressed all in black with a small lace collar came into her bedroom.

Nanny Barstow carefully placed the large armful of freshly ironed clothes she was carrying onto the top of the chest of drawers.

She now took a deep breath and smoothed down the linen apron she was wearing. The endless flights of stairs up from the basement of the tall London house were very steep and she was not getting any younger.

"Now then, my Lady, I've got quite enough to do to get you and your brother packed for your trip to America without fussing about with a perfectly good ball gown."

Nanny Barstow's rather ferocious expression hid a kind and gentle heart.

She had been a lady's maid to Viola's mother and nanny to both Viola and her twin brother, David, since they were born and would cheerfully have laid down her life for both of them without a murmur.

It upset Nanny that her Lady Viola had to wear an old ball gown that had once belonged to her elderly cousin, Miss Edith Matthews.

Miss Matthews owned the house in the big London Square where they were living, but as she wryly told Viola, her ball going days were long past. She was badly crippled by pains in her hips and knees and rarely left her room.

"Now, no more complaining, my Lady. It's so very good of Miss Matthews to let you wear her dress. Now, if I just trim a few of these loose threads from the hem and sleeves and you wear your nice long gloves, it will do very well."

Viola sighed.

"I do wish Papa had sent us some money instead of two boat tickets to New York. I cannot understand why he wants us to visit him. He never has before when he has travelled abroad."

Nanny Barstow sniffed, but did not reply.

Her opinion of the Earl of Northcombe was not one she would repeat to his daughter!

His wife, Helena, had died of pneumonia when the twins were just four years old.

Nanny believed that any normal man would have turned all his attention and affection towards the twins, but the Earl had never seemed interested in his children in any way.

He had very little money of his own and relied on the income from his late wife's investments.

All the family capital was tied up to be inherited by the twins when they reached the age of twenty-one.

For the past number of years, the Earl, who had a restless nature, had plunged into one business scheme after another – always about to make his fortune, but somehow never managing to do so.

If it had not been for the kindness and generosity of Miss Edith Matthews, Nanny had no idea what would have become of the twins.

The Earl had gone out to America two years before and apart from a few infrequent letters, the twins had heard nothing until the tickets had arrived, urging them to travel across the Atlantic and join him in New York as quickly as possible.

"I'll thank you to just let me finish packing your steamer trunk or else you'll never be ready to leave in the morning," Nanny scolded. "Now hurry along, Lady Viola. Your brother has been waiting for you in the drawing room these past twenty minutes."

Viola pinched her already rosy cheeks and picked up her stole.

"Just think, Nanny, this time tomorrow we will be at sea!"

"Hmmph! In my humble opinion, you would have done better having a quiet evening indoors, the pair of you!"

Viola chuckled.

"Oh, Nanny! How you do fuss over us. You know that Charlotte has asked us especially to her birthday ball. There is no way we could have refused to go. She is my best friend in all the world."

Nanny's stern features softened a little.

She did approve of Miss Charlotte Brent and had to admit that the lively young heiress to the Brent fortune had never faltered in her loyal friendship to the Northcombe children, even though they were very poor in comparison with herself.

"Well, make certain you are home at a respectable time. You have to be up early to travel to Southampton."

Viola then kissed Nanny's wrinkled cheek, picked up her wrap and hurried down the steep flights of stairs to the ground floor.

In the drawing room her dear twin brother, David, the Viscount Powell, was sprawled out on the sofa, reading the evening newspaper.

Viola hesitated in the doorway watching him.

She loved David very much. He was slim and tall, but his hair was a darker blond than hers and his eyes were dark grey.

David, shy and retiring, was completely different in character from his far more outgoing sister.

He did not care overmuch for parties or balls. He was a talented artist and his sketches of birds and animals were outstanding.

He was a dreamer and had undoubtedly inherited his father's restlessness, because he longed to travel to the Far East and the more remote islands of the Pacific where he could observe and paint strange birds and butterflies.

Now he looked up and grinned at his sister.

"Thank goodness, Sis! I thought we would arrive at Charlotte's in time for breakfast, you have been so long in getting ready!"

Viola laughed and they hurried out into the street.

Luckily Brent House was situated on the other side of the Square from their cousin's house, so it was easy to walk through the gardens to where carriages and taxis were arriving with the cream of London Society.

"Does this dress look very bad?"

David peered down at his sister.

He had no clear idea of what was or was not 'bad'.

Viola was wearing something creamy and lacy. It smelt a little of mothballs, but he did not think it would be wise to tell her so.

"No, why?"

Viola sighed.

"It belongs to Cousin Edith, that is why! Nanny has packed the only other one I could possibly have worn and, to be fair, that is just as shabby.

"I do wish Papa had sent us some spending money as well as the boat tickets. There are holes in the soles of these shoes and a big darn on the palm of this glove. Oh, I do *so* hate being poor!"

David plucked a pink rosebud from a trailing bush as they passed and pushed it into his buttonhole. He had never known a life when they had had money to spare.

He frowned at Viola.

"Don't you think it odd, Papa asking us to go out to America? I mean, I am delighted we are going. I long to travel the world, as you know, but he has never wanted us to visit him before."

Viola paused as they left the shelter of the garden and stood on the pavement, waiting for a chance to cross the road to the sweeping marble steps of Brent House.

Tall gas torches were flickering brightly on top of ornamental pillars and the big front doors stood wide open to admit the crowds of partygoers.

Viola felt sad when she thought about her father.

5

She realised she was nineteen years old and still did not know him. Indeed she could count on the fingers of one hand the times she had spent more than a fortnight in his company.

But now he wanted his children with him and had sent expensive tickets for berths on a fast cruise liner.

It was all very puzzling as David had remarked.

Well, she would worry about it all when they were on the ship and heading for America.

Tonight she was going to enjoy herself.

She loved dancing and was quite certain that even if she was wearing a perfectly hideous dress, Charlotte would make certain that she danced with plenty of partners.

The great marble entrance hall to Brent House was crowded. Gentlemen in full evening dress escorted ladies resplendent in dazzling gowns, all their jewellery glittering and gleaming in the light from the huge crystal chandelier hanging above them.

David leaned against an imposing marble pillar at one side of the hall, waiting for Viola.

She had been whisked away upstairs by Charlotte Brent, who looked magnificent in a very dark amethyst silk dress, diamonds at her neck and the famous Brent diamond ear-drops plainly on show.

Suddenly David turned and realised that behind the pink and white flower arrangement on a tall pedestal by his side, two dark brown eyes were staring at him.

He moved a stem of white lilies and smiled.

A slender girl, just as tall as his sister, was standing there, her smooth dark hair braided and coiled around her head like a coronet.

She looked nervous and David could see that she was trembling.

"Hello! I say, are you all right there in the middle of all those flowers?"

"Thank you, aye, I am quite all right."

David smiled.

She had a soft Scottish voice.

"I am David – Viscount Powell. How d'y do?"

A small lace gloved hand crept out and touched his fingers for a second.

"Margaret – Lady Margaret Glentorran."

David pushed the flowers to one side.

"Do come out into the hall, Lady Margaret. Or else you will ruin your pretty dress squashed up against those blooms and leaves."

"It was just so noisy! I am not used to so many people. I-I – "

"I know exactly how you feel. But at least it is a cheerful noise. It is just because everyone is so happy and enjoying themselves. Surely you cannot be on your own?"

"Oh, no! I came here with my brother, the Duke of Glentorran. We live up in Scotland – I expect you can tell from my accent. But my brother has business in London with Mr. Brent and so Charlotte's father kindly asked us to her birthday ball.

"But Robert – that is my brother – has gone into the study to converse with Mr. Brent and his City colleagues."

"Well, Lady Margaret, there is no reason for you to stand out here in the hall waiting for him. My sister, Viola, has gone upstairs with Charlotte and if I know them, they will be up there for ages gossiping. What do you say to a dance, while we are waiting for our respective siblings?"

Lady Margaret looked into his kind grey eyes and smiled timidly.

She put her hand on his arm,

"My friends call me 'Meg'."

Upstairs Charlotte and Viola were sitting together in the pretty little anteroom that led from her bedroom.

They had exchanged all the latest information about mutual acquaintances and Viola had exclaimed over her friend's many extravagant birthday presents and Charlotte was fascinated by Viola's forthcoming trip to America.

"Oh, I do wish I was going! It sounds so exciting. And you could meet the man of your dreams on board ship, Viola!"

Viola laughed, her blue eyes sparkling.

She and Charlotte had spoken very many times of the kind of man they would like to marry.

Viola just knew it would have to be someone very special. She did not want a marriage of convenience such as some of her friends had made.

She was sensible enough to recognise that powerful families frequently married their offspring to each other for dynastic reasons, but she wanted to experience the wonder of falling in love and having that love returned.

"The man of my dreams? Goodness, I don't think he exists. I have never met anyone who comes even close to what I would consider to be a man I could really fall in love with!"

Charlotte picked up her perfume bottle and sprayed a fine mist across her shoulders.

Viola glanced admiringly at her beautiful amethyst dress.

"I just love your gown, Charlotte. I must look like a church mouse in this dreadful old rag of Cousin Edith's. Oh, I am so tired of being poor."

Charlotte pulled a face.

She was a most straightforward girl and could not prevaricate and pretend.

Viola's creamy lace gown was certainly awful and did smell of mothballs!

"I say, Viola, I've got an idea. Why don't you wear something of mine? Just for this evening. It would be a great jest. Look – "

She jumped up and threw open a large wardrobe to display a row of wonderful gowns of all colours.

Viola shook her head.

"No, don't be so silly, Charlotte. What would your parents say?"

Charlotte was busy rifling through her dresses.

"Lord, Viola, Mama will not care and Papa won't notice. Look – this one is just made for you. I have only worn it the once. It's not my colour, it's too pale with my complexion, although I love the material."

Viola gasped.

The dress was fashioned from a delightful pale blue gauze, quite low-cut with a deep band of seed pearls and tiny white rosebuds embroidered around the neckline and along the flaring skirt.

It was the most beautiful gown Viola had ever seen and she knew, even before she tried it on, that it would fit her perfectly.

"Oh, Viola. That will look wonderful on you. And see, here is my sapphire necklet. You can wear this, too. It finishes the whole outfit splendidly!"

*

Robert, Duke of Glentorran, came out of the library into the hall and paused.

He needed to find his sister.

He knew she did not care for crowds and noise. He had not intended to leave her on her own for such a long time, but his business discussions with Mr. Brent had been urgent and protracted.

Tall and dark, his face looked stern.

The Duke was deeply worried.

His ancestral Glentorran estate on the West coast of Scotland was in desperate need of money.

The Castle was always referred to locally as a 'little Glamis'. It was very similar in style and design – although much smaller – to the world famous castle near Dundee, where the Earls of Strathmore had lived for centuries.

The Duke loved every inch, every stone, turret and window of his ancient home. He knew all his tenants from the oldest shepherd who tended the flocks on the high hills down to the youngest baby born to one of the fishermen in the village of Glentorran.

But he also recognised that without a considerable investment, he would be forced to close up the Castle and move into the Dower House on the estate.

Hundreds of clansmen completely relied on him for their livelihood and he could see no way of increasing his revenue.

The Duke stood, staring around, trying to find his sister.

He was becoming more and more annoyed by the ceaseless chatter and laughter, the careless gaiety of these Socialites.

Grimly he reckoned that all the jewellery on display this evening would keep his Castle and the estate running for a good twenty years!

Did any of these people know what it was like to be poor?

To have one schoolroom for over fifty children?

For the closest hospital to be miles away across a range of mountains?

What would they know of having responsibility for so many people less fortunate than themselves who had not been born to title and privilege?

He doubted that the people in this house would ever understand.

The Duke strode across the hall and then stopped as a sudden flash of pale blue caught his eye.

The most beautiful girl he had ever seen in his life was gliding down the great stairway towards him.

He did not see the costly dress or even the sparkling sapphires at her neck.

All he could see was the sheer beauty of her face, the proud way she held her head, the tumbled golden curls, carelessly pinned back with a length of cream lace.

He had not the faintest idea who she was or who could introduce him.

Normally the Duke was a quiet reserved man, but some power held him in place at the foot of the stairs and as the angel in blue reached him, he held out his hand and asked her gently,

"Madam, please will you do the honour of dancing with me?"

Viola felt as if she had been swept away into an unknown world.

One second she had been innocently walking down stairs, anxious to show David her marvellous gown and then there was a tall handsome man, holding out his hand, the expression in his dark brown eyes both commanding and imploring at the same time.

With a small gasp she had nodded her acceptance

and now she was held in his arms and they were waltzing, surrounded by light and colour and many people she would undoubtedly know.

But she could see none of them – just the dark eyes that gazed down into hers so intently.

"You will think me amiss, madam, asking you to dance when we have not been introduced. Please allow me to introduce myself. I am Robert, the Duke of Glentorran, at your service."

Viola smiled up at him as he swirled her round, her feet hardly seeming to touch the polished parquet floor.

"Your Grace – I am most delighted to make your acquaintance. I am Lady Viola Northcombe."

"Viola – that is a – "

He hesitated, as he had been about to say, 'that is a beautiful name', but realised he was being far too forward with a young lady he had only just met.

" – interesting name," he finished lamely.

"I can tell from your accent you are from Scotland, Your Grace."

"Aye. The West coast – rugged and heather clad hills, fine beaches and distant mountains. There can be no better place on earth."

Viola sighed.

He spoke of his home with such great warmth and affection. So many men she had met did not care where they lived, as long as it was in comfort and splendour.

"Oh, it sounds so wonderful. I've always longed to live in an old country house. I have dreams of buying an old ruined place and bringing it back to life. I would love to create a wonderful garden that everyone around could enjoy.

She paused.

"Please tell me about Glentorran."

On the other side of the ballroom, Lady Margaret gave a little exclamation of surprise.

"Who can that girl be with my brother? He never dances at balls!"

David spun her round with ease and then laughed.

"Well, though she is wearing a different dress than she set out in earlier this evening, I can tell you that is my twin sister, Viola."

"Your sister?"

"Yes, and please do not say we are not alike. She possesses all the good looks – but I do declare I have all the intelligence!"

A smile glimmered in Lady Margaret's eyes.

"She certainly has some talents to amuse. There – my brother is laughing. That is good to see. He has been so very downcast of late."

Just then the music came to a climax and stopped. Clapping and laughing, the couples moved to the side of the ballroom.

Viola felt she was living in a dream as the Duke led her to a small gilt chair – a dream which she had no wish to awake from.

"Glentorran – "

It was Mr. Brent, Charlotte's father.

"Viola, my dear, you must excuse my interrupting your dance, but I now have some urgent business to discuss with the Duke."

"Can it not wait until later?" the Duke enquired.

"I am afraid not. My colleagues have to leave for the Continent on the night ferry."

The Duke turned, smiled down at Viola and said,

"Please wait here for me. I will be back very soon. If you are not otherwise engaged, perhaps we could take supper together."

"And here is Charlotte to keep you company," Mr. Brent added jovially as his daughter swept across the floor towards them.

Viola watched him closely as the Duke bowed and walked away with his host.

Her head was spinning with pictures of lochs and heather, mountains and sheep shearing, tartans and rivers bounding with salmon.

The Duke loved his country so much and he was a fascinating man.

She could not remember ever meeting anyone she had been so attracted to from the very beginning.

Could this possibly be the man of her dreams?

And – her heart gave a little jump –

He seemed to like her as well.

"Are you enjoying wearing the blue gown?" asked Charlotte, sinking into a chair next to Viola and fanning herself vigorously.

"The blue – oh, I had quite forgotten!"

Charlotte laughed.

"You've obviously been having a good time. Did I see you dancing with the Duke of Glentorran?"

Viola bent over the pearl buttons on her glove. She did not want Charlotte to comment on the blush she knew was staining her cheeks.

"Yes – he asked me for the waltz and we spoke of Scotland."

"Oh, that draughty old castle of his! That's all he ever talks about. He was here for luncheon yesterday with

14

his sister and it was obvious that he cannot wait to get back to the Highlands."

"Why are they in London?"

Charlotte gazed around the busy ballroom, seeking her next partner.

"What? Oh, Mama told me that he is looking for a rich wife."

Viola felt the blood drain from her face.

"A rich wife?" she whispered.

"Why, yes. Goodness, Viola, you know how much money these huge Scottish estates eat up. He needs a lot of money very quickly, and the fastest way of achieving it is to marry an heiress, or a girl with plenty of money that he can use to his own advantage. I say, my sapphires really suit you. Mama says I should wear emeralds, but – "

But Viola was no longer listening.

Her world lay shattered around her.

She fingered the pale blue gauze of Charlotte's skirt and then touched the warm stones that lay against her skin.

So that was why the Duke had seemed to like her so much!

She gave every impression of being rich!

A man of the world, such as he, would have known immediately that the diamond necklet she was wearing was worth a small fortune.

He would probably even realise that the beautiful dress had cost more than a working man could earn in six months.

He had come to London to look for a rich wife – and thought he had found a likely candidate.

Viola felt a wave of bitterness and disappointment sweep over her.

She had liked him so much.

The man of her dreams!

That was exactly what she had begun to think.

What a fool she was!

Well, she would show him that she cared nothing for him or his Scottish estate.

Robert, the Duke of Glentorran, walked back into the ballroom half an hour later, feeling deeply disappointed by his business meeting.

He had been able to borrow a meagre amount from the City gentlemen he had just been introduced to, but not nearly sufficient to repair the Castle roof and some of the tenants' crofts.

The whole visit to London had turned into a failure – except for one thing – meeting Lady Viola Northcombe.

That wonderful girl was worth every minute he had been forced to stay here in the South.

He glanced over to where he had left her, knowing that she would have waited for him.

But the gilt chair was occupied by someone else.

Scowling he glanced round the room.

There was his sister, Margaret, dancing with a tall blond young man. She seemed happy, for which he was thankful, realising he had neglected her for the past hour.

But he wanted to find his angel girl.

Surely Viola's blue dress would be easy to spot – *there*!

Then, as he watched her, his face grew dark and his emotions tumbled into turmoil.

Lady Viola was sitting in a little alcove, surrounded by attentive young men.

She was drinking champagne, laughing loudly and

openly flirting, the lovely sapphire necklet sparkling as she moved.

The Duke observed several older ladies giving her scandalous glances at they passed.

He just could not believe that it was the same quiet beauty who had stolen his heart earlier that evening.

With a thunderous expression on his face, he strode through the crowd.

All he wanted to do now was to collect his sister and leave.

He wished to go home, back to Scotland where rich young women did not play silly games with men they had just met.

He hesitated as he approached Viola, then stopped, bowed his head curtly, ignoring the flush of embarrassment his offhand actions might cause her and strode on to snatch a bewildered protesting Margaret away from her partner.

Viola watched him go, her heart sinking in despair.

'Good riddance,' she fumed to herself, placing the champagne glass she had pretended to empty onto a table.

She stood up and signalled to David.

All she desired too was to go home and leave this house where the man of her dreams had just turned out to be a fortune-hunting rogue.

But even as she and David walked silently back across the Square, she found herself wishing she had not behaved in such a frivolous way and that she had explained herself to the Duke in a frank and sensible fashion.

Viola sighed.

Tomorrow they would set sail for America and she knew she was unlikely ever to meet the Duke of Glentorran again.

CHAPTER TWO

Robert, Duke of Glentorran, was clambering down the steep rocky steps that had been cut into the cliff face by his ancestors years many centuries ago.

It was a wild day for early June.

The sea was crashing onto the sharp black rocks of the West coast of Scotland in great walls of white foam and dark grey-green water.

The early summer storm was blowing fierce clouds in from the far horizon, shutting out the sun.

It was a day that matched the Duke's mood – black and miserable.

The sharp pebbles of the little cove crunched under his boots as he strode down to the water's edge, his dark green kilt swinging around his knees.

He stared out across the ocean, allowing the cold salty wind to blow his dark hair into wild tangles.

High above him, on the cliffs of Glentorran, stood his home, the Castle he loved so much.

He knew every inch of its endless corridors, turrets and rooms. He had explored all the cellars and attics since his childhood and could recognise every stone and tile that made up the amazing building that looked so much like its bigger Royal relation, Glamis Castle.

He had inherited the Castle and estate on the death of his ne'er-do-well father, Kenneth.

The Glentorran estate consisted of miles of heather-covered hills where big herds of deer roamed, sheep farms, fishing villages and little crofts that eked a living out of the hard ground.

The Duke had always believed that the Castle and the estate were only temporarily his on trust, handed down to him by generations of the Glentorran family.

His to hold until he could pass them on to a son.

He picked up a handful of stones from the beach and threw them, one by one, out across the waves that were now hissing around his feet.

He felt a great weight on his shoulders.

He believed he had failed in his duty.

The Castle and the estate were now in great danger of being lost to the Glentorrans.

The majority of the money his father had left had been eaten up by paying the late Duke's massive gambling debts.

He knew that if he could not raise sufficient money quickly, he would be forced to sell the Castle and the estate and abandon the people who looked to him for leadership and support.

He had even tried asking the hard-hearted London City men for a large loan just a few months ago, but that had failed miserably.

Now he did not know which way to turn.

His thoughts were as stormy as the clouds above, but he tried to smile as he heard the pebbles of the beach crunch behind him.

His dear sister, Margaret, or Meg as he had always called her, was now walking towards him, her thick knitted shawl wrapped tightly around her thin shoulders to protect her from the wind and rain.

She linked her arm through his and briefly touched her dark head to his shoulder.

"Cheer up, Robert. I know you are worried, but I am sure you will find a way to save the estate."

Her brother gave her a brief hug.

"If I only knew you were settled, it would help a great deal, Meg. I can fend for myself, but I do not want to see you reduced to poverty."

She laughed.

"Och, Robert, you *do* exaggerate. We will always have enough to live on. We can close the Castle and move to the Dower House. I will sell my jewellery and we can farm and fish and I will grow vegetables for the pot!"

The Duke's brow furrowed.

His little sister had such a romantic view of life.

They lived economically as it was, but every luxury would vanish if they lost the Castle.

Admittedly Meg's lovely jewellery would bring in some money, but how could he possibly ask her to sell her inheritance?

"If only you were married – "

The Duke's voice died away.

'If only' were two very sad words.

He knew he could never force his sister to marry without love, because that was something he would never do himself.

Ever since he had become an adult, he had longed to find that one very special girl to whom he could give his heart, completely and utterly.

He knew that people expected him to find a wealthy wife whose money he could use to his own advantage, but he could never countenance such a gesture.

No, he knew he could only marry for love and even if he found her, he could never marry when the future was so uncertain.

He closed his mind to thoughts of the slim blonde girl he had danced with in London.

Because he knew that, whatever he might be telling himself, he would have asked her to marry him, regardless of what fate held in store.

However, he had fallen foul of his own imagination where she was concerned and he knew that if they ever did meet again, she would certainly have no inclination to take their friendship any further.

Lady Margaret sighed deeply as she tied her shawl tightly around her shoulders as a gust of wind tried to send it spiralling into the rain.

She recognised that she did not have the outgoing, sparkling personality that most young men looked for in a wife.

And all the local eligible bachelors were extremely wary of taking on the impoverished sister of Glentorran in case they were asked to pour their own family's funds into the estate.

Mind you, she had never met anyone she wanted to marry – then she hesitated, her mind whirling back to an evening several months ago, when she had been dancing with David, the Viscount Powell.

She had never met a man like him before in her life – someone whose mind was so similar to her own.

She shook her head to clear her thoughts.

That particular evening had ended badly and there was no reason to imagine she would ever meet the young Viscount again.

The Duke was peering through the mist and spray, out to sea.

"Look – there's a big boat out there, Meg, beyond the rocks! Not one of our fishing fleet, thank God, who are all tucked up at anchor safely in harbour. I do not envy those passengers on a day such as this."

"I wonder where they are headed? We are a long way from the shipping lanes here."

"Well, if we do not get indoors, we will be as wet as those poor sailors. Come, Meg, I have some crofters coming to speak to me about repairs to their homes. It is not going to be a pleasant meeting."

And they turned away from the stormy ocean and distant boat and began the steep ascent up the slippery rock steps back to the grounds of Glentorran Castle.

*

On board the luxury motor yacht *Stars and Stripes*, Lady Viola Northcombe fought her way against the raging wind along the companionway to the luxurious lounge.

The violent movement of the vessel had sent most of the other passengers into their cabins, but Viola had not felt a moment's sickness since they had left New York.

Her brother David was sitting wedged into a corner of one of the long benches.

He was shivering violently and looked desperately pale and ill. His fine blond hair fell across his forehead in a sweat-dampened tangle and even as she looked at him, he was racked by a fit of coughing.

"David, you should go below! Get into your bunk and sleep."

"In this sea? No, thanks, Sis, I would far rather be up here where there is some fresh air. Oh, but I am so cold! I wish we could reach land. I want to sleep in a bed that doesn't move. I am sure I would feel better then and get rid of this dreadful cough."

Viola bit her lip, pulled off the heavy coat she was wearing and laid it across him.

"Here – let me tuck this coat round you. The storm cannot last for long – Captain Howard assures me that we will outrun it soon."

Viola sat next to David and held his hand tightly as the boat rolled and pitched.

This journey across the Atlantic had started out so well, but it had turned into a nightmare.

The first part of their trip from New York to Dublin had gone smoothly.

The other passengers were quiet interesting people and Viola had enjoyed their company.

The crew had proved attentive and polite and Viola had felt vindicated in her decision to sail home on a small boat rather than wait for her brother to regain his strength.

David had spent much of his time in his cabin and Viola had begun to be increasingly worried about her twin. She felt he should be further along the road to recovery than he was.

They had docked briefly in Belfast where several of the passengers had disembarked.

Then the boat had immediately set out on the short journey across the Irish Sea towards Liverpool.

"This is totally different to our wonderful journey outbound to America," murmured David, his voice low and hoarse.

Viola smiled.

It had been a fantastic trip on a great liner, although she had still been smarting from her brief encounter with the Duke of Glentorran.

But she had been determined to enjoy herself and had forced herself to dance every night, in spite of a desire to sit and ruminate over the dark-haired Scotsman who had annoyed her so much.

However, all the excitement of the voyage over had paled into insignificance when they reached America.

The first clue that their lives were about to change was the luxurious chauffeur-driven car that awaited them at the quayside in New York.

They were hurried past the necessary officials by a young man who announced that he was to be their personal assistant and they were next driven to a vast house in the most expensive part of New York.

Inside the opulent mansion they were greeted by a tall thick-set American, Mr. Lewis Wilder.

Viola had noticed at once that he was wearing black and his square rugged face carried a sad expression.

But she could never have dreamed of what he was about to tell them.

Tragically their father had died of a fever just four days before they reached New York!

David was now the new Earl of Northcombe and this vast house belonged to them.

But that was not all.

The rest of Lewis Wilder's news was so incredible that even now Viola could scarcely believe how much their fortunes had changed.

Because they had now become amazingly rich – so wealthy it made her head spin.

She had seen the figures laid out before her in the bank manager's office and realised that from now on she could buy what she liked and never miss it.

But even so, it still seemed totally unreal, as if she had fallen asleep in Cousin Edith's house in London and was dreaming the whole adventure.

Now as the motor yacht they were travelling home in tossed violently in the storm, she said to her brother,

"At least we can pay for the very best treatment for you when we land."

David smiled weakly.

"All I want is rest, quiet, warmth and really good English food, Sis. I enjoyed America, but everywhere was so noisy."

"I still find it hard to believe that Papa finally made his fortune finding oil, when he had spent all those years when we were both young, chasing one foolish dream after another," sighed Viola.

"At least he lived long enough to know he was rich and that his children would never need for anything again."

"But at the cost of his life! Remember that Lewis Wilder told us how our poor Papa contracted the fever that killed him down in Texas in the oil fields."

David coughed, his whole body shaking. He pulled Viola's thick warm coat closer to his chin.

"I wish I could feel some sun on my face! Listen, Viola, I like to think that our Papa would have felt that his life's work was finished. He had achieved everything he had set out to do and was at last vindicated in the eyes of everyone who said he was a fool and a dreamer!"

Viola nodded.

It was increasingly difficult to recall those first few weeks in America as the days had passed in such a whirl of activity.

She had been sad to lose her father, of course, but if she was honest, she had seen him so little in the course of her life that it was like hearing of the passing of a distant relation.

Viola was sorry, but not heartbroken.

"Wilder was not pleased when we said we wanted to return home to England," David said shrewdly. "I have a distinct feeling that he would like to become more than your business partner, my dear Sis! I caught him looking at you at times and there was rather more in his expression than admiration from a mere colleague!"

Viola blushed and turned to gaze out of a porthole at the angry grey seas.

Lewis Wilder, had, indeed, become something of a trial in the last month of their stay in New York.

At first she and David had been grateful for all his help.

He had been their father's partner and as such he introduced them to the staff of their new home, to lawyers and bank managers and explained about the oil fields they now owned between them.

Lewis Wilder had supported the bewildered brother and sister through the trauma of their father's funeral and arranged for flowers and announcements in the newspapers both in America and back home in England.

He had a wide circle of friends in New York, all of whom were eager to meet the young English aristocrats.

After several weeks of mourning Viola and David had found themselves with a busy and exciting social life, helped by all the money they could possibly spend.

"You are quite right. He did ask me to marry him," replied Viola. "That was one of the reasons I wanted to go home so badly. I found being constantly in his company was becoming extremely disagreeable."

David coughed again.

"Sorry, Sis, my falling ill did rather slow us down. I hope that Wilder didn't make too much of a nuisance of himself while I was laid up?"

Viola shook her blonde head, feeling reluctant to bother him with reports of how offensive the big American had actually been.

He had made it very clear that if they were married, he would then have the power her money would give him to build up a vast oil-producing empire in the South-West of America.

There had been a dreadful scene when she refused his proposal and although he had called at the mansion the next day and apologised to her, Viola was quite certain he was only pretending to be sorry.

Lewis Wilder was a man who always got what he wanted. Powerful and arrogant, he could be very charming when he chose to be.

Viola felt strangely threatened by him and although she knew that he could not marry her against her wishes, she made up her mind to return home to England.

But just as they had both decided to leave America, David had been caught in a heavy rainstorm while he was out sketching and had developed pneumonia.

For a long week Viola had remained by her twin's bedside, doing her best to help the doctor and nurses, living in dread that he would not survive.

But luckily God had listened to her fervent prayers and thankfully David had pulled through, although he was still extremely weak.

As soon as she was convinced that he was over the worst of his illness, Viola had booked passage on a liner heading for Britain.

But when she told him of her arrangements, David had said he was sorry, but he could not face all the people, the size of the ship and the hustle and bustle of an Atlantic crossing.

Fortunately it was then that Viola had heard that the Van Ashtons, acquaintances of theirs, who owned a large, luxurious, ocean-going motor yacht, were preparing to sail for England on holiday.

It was to be a small party – three couples with their staff and the crew of the yacht.

Mrs. Van Ashton, a large lady who was delighted to be friends with a *real* English Earl and his sister, had been thrilled when Viola asked if she and her brother could join the yacht and readily agreed to take them.

They steamed majestically out of New York for the Atlantic crossing, little knowing what the spring weather would hold for them.

"Well, Lewis Wilder is out of your life now," said David one afternoon while he and Viola settled into a quiet corner of the yacht's grandiose Saloon well away from the strong wind and rough sea outside.

"He will continue to manage the businesses over in America and there is no need for us to meet again unless he comes to England.

"Once we land, we can set about our own plans for the future. Buy a house – pay back Cousin Edith in some way – oh, and we will now be able to take care of Nanny as well!"

"Which part of the country shall we live in?" asked Viola dreamily.

David shrugged.

"I shall leave that decision to you, Sis. Once I am well and strong again, I intend to roam all over the world. I shall take my sketchbook and journey to all the odd and exciting places that I have heard so much about and never thought I would ever see."

Viola smiled at him.

In some ways, he was so like their father, always wanting to see and do something new. Although luckily he had no taste for the business world or gambling.

"I shall buy a house in London and another one in the country," Viola decided emphatically. "You shall come and go as you wish and I will frame all your sketches and hang them everywhere for people to admire."

She stood up just as the boat gave a great heave and corkscrewed around before crashing down into the water again.

Viola was flung up against the wall and managed to catch hold of the curtains that hung at the porthole.

"Good Heavens, David! I can see land!"

"What? You can't possibly, Sis. We are nowhere near land – "

Viola craned her head to see through the foam and spray crashing against the glass.

"But I can! There are dark hills and a flashing light. Oh, David, look! There are rocks! I can see them clearly."

Her brother struggled to his feet, pushing her coat to the floor and joined her at the porthole.

"My word! You are so right. Something has gone badly wrong, Viola, that is definitely not the coastline near Liverpool! This storm must have blown us miles off our course."

Suddenly the ship's siren started to sound wildly and then there was the sound of shouting and many feet running.

Above the shriek of the wind a loud crash sounded and the boat seemed to quiver all over.

An ear-splitting grating noise shattered through the storm as the ship tilted violently to one side.

"We've hit the rocks!" groaned David. "Quickly, Viola. We must get to the lifeboat."

They forced their way out onto the deck where the crew were shouting, the Captain bellowing orders and all was noise and chaos.

Mrs. Van Ashton appeared in disarray, clinging to her husband's arm and moaning.

Her little maid scurried along behind her, clutching a vast jewellery box in her arms.

Viola had a sudden fleeting thought that thousands of pounds worth of diamonds were about to be lost in the icy waters that pounded against the sides of the ship.

Captain Howard made his way gingerly along the tilting deck.

"My Lord, Lady Viola, I am sorry to say we have hit some vicious rocks and the ship's hull has been holed in several places! Luckily people ashore have seen us. They have signalled to us by lantern.

"We are taking on water, but slowly. I can launch the ship's lifeboat on the port side, but not the one on the starboard, which is the one that you and my Senior Officers would use.

"I think we will be best advised to wait for a boat to reach us from the shore rather than try to launch the second lifeboat when we are tilting so badly – "

Viola clung to the brass railing along the deck and peered towards the coast which was shrouded in mist.

She could see a few blurred lights in the distance.

"We will go by your advice, Captain Howard," said David. "We do not seem very far from land. How can this have happened?"

The Captain looked grim.

"I have no idea, my Lord, but I assure you I intend to find out. Now, if you will excuse me, I must oversee the rest of the passengers."

Viola and David stood close together on the steeply sloping deck, watching while the first lifeboat was lowered and the other passengers scrambled aboard.

Suddenly Viola could hear shouting from the water close by.

She peered over the edge as a rowing boat appeared out of the mist close to the ship.

There was a young man at the oars with his red hair plastered to his head by the driving rain, his strong arms effortlessly powering the boat forward.

Another man was standing in the prow, balancing himself with ease as the waves tossed the boat around. He was wearing a dark rain jacket and had a fisherman's hat pulled down as far as his shoulders.

He waved imperiously at Viola and David as he shouted up to the deck,

"You need to jump now! The ship's beginning to settle."

"You go first, David!"

"Certainly not! Jump, Viola. I'll be right behind you."

Viola swung herself over the rail, balanced for a second or two and then let herself drop down towards the man in the rowing boat.

Strong arms caught hold of her and for a minute they swayed together as the boat rocked under her weight.

"Thank you! Thank you *so* much!"

Viola tilted her head back to look up at her rescuer and then gulped.

He pushed his floppy hat back from his sodden face and she instantly recognised the stern dark face of Robert, the Duke of Glentorran.

CHAPTER THREE

"*You*!"

Robert, the Duke of Glentorran, gazed down at the face that had haunted his dreams for months.

The same dark blue eyes and perfect mouth.

Although her long hair was darkened to amber by the driving rain and spray, he would have recognised her anywhere.

"Your Grace – "

Viola's voice was no more than a whisper.

She could not think clearly, especially as the Duke was still holding her tightly in his arms as the little rowing boat swayed alarmingly in the rough sea.

For a long second they just stared into each other's eyes and then the Duke gave his head a little shake.

"We will talk later," he grunted abruptly whilst he helped her to a seat.

"My brother, sir. He has not been well. He is very weak. I don't know if he can manage to jump down into this boat."

Viola stared up to where David was leaning against the ship's railing far above her head.

But not that far now!

The luxurious vessel was slowly sinking.

Without another word, the Duke swung himself up a rope hanging over the side of the ship and helped David clamber down it.

He eased him safely into the rowing boat, frowning as he saw the young man's white face.

David was now shaking violently and looked half-unconscious and desperately ill.

"How many more are still left on board?" the Duke shouted to Viola above the howling of the wind.

She wiped spray from her eyes.

"The Captain and some of his crew, Your Grace."

Just then another rowing boat appeared through the mist and the Duke shouted in a strange language to the men manning its oars.

Then he turned to his red-headed companion.

"They will take the Captain and his crew to safety. Row us to shore, Fergus. To the Castle, not the harbour. As fast as you can. I must get the Viscount into the warm."

"Viscount no longer," murmured Viola. "Our father has died and David is now the Earl of Northcombe."

The Duke nodded.

"My deep condolences, Lady Viola. But whatever his title, he needs to be in a warm bed very quickly with a doctor in full attendance. *Why* on earth did you allow him to travel in this state?"

Viola tossed her head at the reproof in his voice.

Was this man just always going to find fault with everything she did? At least *she* was not trying to marry for money!

"I thought the time of year, late May, meant that the sea would be calm. David had recovered from pneumonia – our doctor in America said that he was fit to travel. But sadly he seems to have suffered a major relapse in the last few days."

She bent over her twin, trying to protect him from the worst of the rain.

Her heavy coat had been left behind on the sinking yacht along with all their clothes and possessions, she now realised.

But at least they were now safe and that was all that mattered.

Five minutes later the rowing boat was grounding on the stony shore of a little cove.

With the Duke on one side and Fergus on the other, David was helped from the boat and half-led, half-carried up the steep stone steps cut into the cliff face.

Viola bent down and gathered up her soaking skirt, the heavy woollen fabric made much heavier by cold sea water, and followed behind them, fighting hard to keep her balance on the slippery surface.

The Duke turned when they were halfway up.

"Can you manage, Lady Viola?"

"Yes, certainly. See to David, please."

Without another word, the Duke now reached down a tanned hand and pulled her up a particularly steep step.

Then he returned his attention to the young Earl.

As they reached the top of the steps, Viola looked up and gasped.

There in front of her, the mist drifting around it like white chiffon scarves, stood Glentorran Castle, its pointed turrets, tall chimneys and wonderful deep windows giving it a magical appearance.

"Oh, how wonderful!"

The words of delight fell from Viola's lips before she could stop them.

"How incredibly beautiful!"

The Duke's stern face relaxed slightly.

It was odd how happy her words made him.

"Aye – it's a bonny place. And it will stay bonny for a good while yet! There will be plenty of time for you to explore. Ah, here comes my sister!"

Lady Margaret Glentorran now came flying down the pathway that led from a rough shrubbery area, her long black hair loose around her shoulders.

"I have alerted Mrs. Livesey – there are beds to be prepared – and – oh, my goodness!"

She clasped her hands to her mouth.

"I just *cannot* believe it. It is David! I mean it is Lord Powell and Lady Viola!"

"It most certainly is, Meg, but for now all questions and explanations must wait. This young man is not well. Please go back to the house and send Euan for the doctor immediately."

Lady Margaret hesitated for a moment, not wishing to leave David's side, but then obedience to her brother's order overcame her inclinations and so she turned and sped away, her tartan shawl flying behind her in the rain.

The Duke and Fergus now bundled David through the grounds and into the Castle.

A great arched stone corridor led past the kitchens, the staff quarters and the back staircases to the baize door that divided the two parts of the Castle.

After another long passage, they reached the Great Hall of the Castle where Margaret was waiting with a grey-haired older woman dressed in black, a large cameo brooch fastening a piece of fine white lace to the neck of her dress.

"Och, the poor young gentleman. Fergus, take him up the stairs to the Green room at once. Lady Margaret will show you the way. I have rung for the doctor, Your Grace, and there is a warming pan in the bed and cook is sending up beef broth."

"Thank you, Mrs. Livesey. Fergus please carry him gently upstairs. Lady Viola – this is Mrs. Dorcas Livesey, our housekeeper here at the Castle for many years. As was her mother before her and her mother before that! There have always been Liveseys at Glentorran."

"Welcome, my Lady. I have a room ready for you as well, next door to your brother's. I have had a fire lit because even in early summer, Scotland can be very chilly in the evening.

"I will lead the way if you would kindly follow me. You need to change out of those wet clothes quickly or we will have two invalids on our hands!"

"I will wait for the doctor," said the Duke and must have caught Viola's expression of surprise.

"I am afraid the staff at the Castle have been much reduced of late and Euan, who is the one and only footman, has been sent to summon the medical help."

"We do not wish to be a nuisance – " Viola began. "Perhaps a local hotel could – "

The Duke waved away her words with a brusque,

"Och, what rubbish! Never let it be said anywhere that Glentorran hospitality is lacking in any way!"

Viola dropped a brief bob of gratitude and followed the housekeeper up the narrow winding staircase that led to the upper levels of the Castle.

Her room was rather small, the dark green curtains and carpet clean, but worn and old-fashioned.

Viola pulled off her soaking clothes, glad to find an old silk quilted dressing gown hanging behind the door.

She pulled her hair free from its pins and rubbed it as dry as she could in the towel provided for her.

Then she sank down on the bed and buried her face in her hands.

The relief of eventually being safe, the worry over David's health and having to face the Duke of Glentorran suddenly overwhelmed her.

She closed her eyes gratefully and fell instantly into a deep sleep from sheer exhaustion.

*

A few hours later she awoke feeling much stronger.

Someone must have come unheard into her room while she was asleep, because an oil lamp had been lit and glowed gently on the dressing table whilst a large fire was crackling in the grate.

In the passageway outside her room, she could hear muffled voices and guessed that the doctor had arrived.

Wrapping the quilted dressing gown firmly around her slender waist, she opened the door and stepped out.

A thin wiry gentleman with sparse, sandy-coloured hair and bushy eyebrows in a dark old-fashioned frock coat was standing there talking to Lady Margaret.

"Och, Lady Viola, you are awake! Excellent. This is Doctor Monroe. He has been examining your brother."

"Good evening doctor. How is David? I have been so worried about him."

Doctor Monroe turned shrewd blue eyes on her.

"Good evening to you, Lady Viola. Well now, yon brother of yours, he is not as fit as a young man should be, and that is the truth of the matter."

"But he is in no danger, surely?"

Viola was overcome with guilt.

If anything dreadful was to happen to her beloved David, she would blame herself. They should have stayed much longer in America until he was fully recovered from his pneumonia.

It was only her silly fancy to get away from Lewis Wilder and his marriage demands that had made her want to flee in such a stupid headstrong fashion.

"Don't fret yourself, my Lady. With good nursing and good food, he should pull through. But he will need to be kept warm and quiet for several weeks or I will not be answering for the consequences."

Viola bit her lip.

"But, doctor, we must travel down to London. We cannot possibly stay here in Scotland. Why, we only have with us the clothes we are standing up in and no money nor possessions of any sort."

Doctor Monroe picked up his black bag and peered at the two girls over his little square spectacles.

"I thought I had made myself clear, Lady Viola, but I will say it once more. Yon young Lord is not to be moved from this Castle for at least a month! And that is my final word on the matter. Now I will wish you a good evening. I will see myself out, Lady Margaret, and I will return to examine my patient in a day or two."

Viola gazed helplessly at Lady Margaret whilst the doctor vanished down the corridor towards the stairs.

"This is just *awful*. How could we possibly impose on your brother's hospitality for such a long time?"

A look of concern crossed Lady Margaret's pretty face.

"It is no imposition on us at all. I am quite sure that Robert would be shocked to hear that you thought it so."

Viola's head was whirling.

She knew the Scottish girl was right, but how could she possibly manage to exist under the same roof as the Duke for a whole month when they had parted on such bad terms in London?

"And Lady Viola – "

"Oh, please call me Viola."

Lady Margaret blushed.

"Why thank you. And everyone here calls me Meg. Margaret seemed such a big name when I was a wee child!

"I was about to suggest, don't worry yourself about clothes. Although you are slightly taller than me, I am sure there will be no problem in altering some of my dresses so they will fit you. And I do know that Robert has plenty of kilts. When your brother is able to move around, I am sure that he will look fine in a kilt!"

Viola smiled to herself as she imagined the look of horror that would cross her twin brother's face when faced with wearing what he would consider a *skirt*!

"Mrs. Livesey is sitting in with your brother at the moment, but obviously you will wish to see him straight away.

"I'll be away and find you some garments to wear tomorrow. I have also arranged for a meal to be served in your bedroom, as I am sure you do not want to be bothered with formal dining tonight."

Viola thanked her profusely, deeply impressed by how well organised she was.

At first glance Lady Margaret seemed rather a shy timid creature, but this was obviously not the case.

She entered David's room, her mind still spinning.

Clearly they would have to stay in Scotland for at least a month.

Viola had no idea how the Duke would react to that particular piece of news!

*

The next morning a sharp fresh wind blew through Viola's open window.

She awoke warm and comfortable and then sprang out of bed to gaze from the casement window, wondering at the beauty of the wild rocky coastline that lay spread out before her.

The storms of the day before had vanished and the sky was a pale eggshell blue and the sea a flat plate of dark green.

Viola realised her room was high up in one of the turrets and she could see for miles in both directions.

On one side of the turret a window looked out over acres of neglected grounds that lead towards the moors and distant mountains.

From the window on the other side of her room the view was of the sea.

And there, only a few short yards from the beach – that must be the ring of vicious rocks that had been their ship's downfall.

There was no sign of wreckage anywhere and she imagined it must have sunk without a trace.

Turning back to her room she found underclothes, a long-sleeved white blouse and a freshly pressed tweed skirt and jacket hanging on a hook behind the door.

Someone had indeed been busy overnight because when she put on the skirt, it fitted perfectly.

The shoes she had worn had been dried and cleaned and she washed and dressed with speed, anxious to check on how her brother had passed the night.

Viola spent only moments tying back her long fair hair with a piece of ribbon she had discovered in one of the dressing table drawers. It was bright red and far too gaudy, but she did not think that anyone was going to criticise her today.

Opening David's door, she peered in cautiously and found he was still fast asleep.

Mrs. Livesey was sitting in a chair next to the bed, also dozing.

David looked pale, certainly, but Viola thought his breathing seemed easier than the day before and a flood of relief raced through her.

She tiptoed out of the room without waking either nurse or patient and made her way down the steep winding staircase into the Great Hall.

The front door – heavy and intimidating, made out of nail-studded oak – was standing ajar and Viola could not resist slipping out into the fresh air.

She gasped in delight as before her lay the tumble of overgrown gardens and then the mauve of heather clad moors swept up and away towards the imposing mountains in the very far distance.

"Oh, what a *wonderful* sight!"

"I am so glad you think so."

Viola spun round.

The Duke of Glentorran was standing behind her, a smile warming his normally stern dark face.

Clad in an old green jersey and riding breeches, he held out his hand to Viola.

"Good morning, Lady Viola. I do hope you slept well."

"Thank you, Your Grace. I did indeed."

"And your brother? I have not yet had a chance to speak to Mrs. Livesey about him."

"He is still asleep, but he looks a little better to me. Your Grace – I am very sorry we have to impose ourselves on your most generous hospitality in this way. I would have liked to make arrangements for us to travel to London today, but the doctor has assured me – "

The Duke held up a commanding hand.

"Stop at once please! Not another word. I am only too pleased to be of service. And I know Meg is delighted to make your brother's acquaintance once again, but I only wish that it was under happier circumstances."

"Have you heard any news of our fellow travellers and the crew of the ship?"

The Duke nodded his head and clicked his fingers at two spaniels, who were sitting patiently at the bottom of the steps waiting for him.

"A message arrived late last night from the village. They are all well fortunately. The Captain and his men are to report to Glasgow to speak to Officials there. The others are travelling to London today, I believe."

"Oh, that is a great relief."

He smiled.

"Would you care for a short walk before breakfast? The view of the Castle is very fine from that small hill over yonder."

Viola nodded her agreement and, side by side, they made their way down the steps and through a wilderness of overgrown shrubbery and flower beds.

The late spring flowers were still in bloom.

Viola frowned as she saw tulips and lilies trying to force their way through heavy weeds and brambles.

The Duke noticed her expression.

"Yes, I'm afraid that the gardens have indeed fallen into poor repair lately. Meg does try to manage – she has a canny vegetable plot on the other side of the stables – but this was our mother's greatest pride and joy – her flower garden. We are not experts and our old gardener is finding it a sad trial."

He whistled to the dogs that were rooting under a bush for rabbits and then continued,

"I am afraid Glentorran has fallen on hard times. I cannot afford to keep a staff of four or five men any longer just to work in the gardens."

Viola was about to comment how difficult he must find it running a large estate such as his, when he went on with a quiet intensity in his voice,

"I do have to apologise most profusely to you, Lady Viola. My behaviour when we first met in London was not that of a gentleman."

"Oh, I have long forgotten all about that," she cried. "So much has happened since then. You see, my father – "

"Your good friend, Charlotte Brent, told me in no uncertain terms a day later that you and your brother are in the same circumstances as myself and Meg! Two brothers and sisters both fallen on hard times! She explained to me that you had even borrowed that expensive dress you were wearing as well as the fabulous sapphire necklet."

He laughed suddenly.

"Why, if you had indeed owned that fabulous piece of jewellery, I might well be asking you for a loan instead of the bankers!"

Viola listened quietly to his words.

They had left the overgrown garden behind by now and were climbing the track that wound around the side of the hill, leading up towards the moors.

The wind was sweet and clean in her face and she could hear dozens of oystercatchers and curlews calling as they swooped over the heather.

The Scottish air tasted like wine.

Here at Glentorran was such a long way away from the glittering heated ballroom where they had first met.

She risked a sideways glance at the Duke, who was whistling for his dogs to come to heel.

Although everything had changed dramatically for her and David, his life remained the same, difficult and still full of problems.

How could she possibly tell him about their good fortune? That the Earl of Northcombe and his sister Viola were now fabulously rich?

And she could buy several sapphire necklets if she so chose.

'But you must tell him!' she thought swiftly. 'You cannot possibly live under his roof for a month under such false pretences. That would be – *cheating*.'

But as she was about to open her mouth to speak, the Duke caught her arm and spun her round.

"There! Isn't that the most beautiful sight you have ever seen?"

Viola gulped in amazement.

They were high enough to look down on Glentorran Castle where it sat on its prominent headland, the deep blue sea behind it, the turrets and chimneys making it look like a picture from a child's story book.

"It is truly breathtaking. You must be extremely proud of it."

The Duke ran his fingers through his tousled black hair.

"We are taught as children that pride is a bad thing. But I am proud of my country and my land. The Dukes of Glentorran have lived and worked here for centuries. I will do anything to keep the Castle and the estate intact for my heirs. *Anything*! It is my sacred duty."

Viola caught her breath.

Suddenly she could recall Charlotte's words, telling her that the Duke was hunting for a rich wife – that he *had* to marry money in order to save Glentorran.

Oh, she so wanted the Duke to like her for herself, for who she was, not for what she possessed.

And how would she ever know his true opinion of her if he once discovered that she was wealthy? She would never believe that he did not pay her attention because of her money and what it could buy.

They turned round and made their way back down the track – the Duke calling to the dogs, talking cheerfully of breakfast and wondering if her brother was awake and able to receive visitors.

Viola answered him automatically, her mind totally occupied elsewhere.

She had made her decision and it was too late now to go back on it.

She and David would have to stay here in Scotland for a month until he was well enough to travel.

Then they would leave and the Duke would never need to know about the fortune they had inherited.

She hastened her steps as they reached the Castle once more.

It was vital that she spoke to David before he met with the Duke.

Viola was certain that her twin had not been in any state the previous night to talk about their life in America, but at any moment he could disclose the truth.

And that was something she could *not* allow.

No, David must swear to her that he would tell no one about their fortune.

CHAPTER FOUR

Viola left her brother's bedroom and hurried back into her own to tidy up her wind-tossed hair before making her way down the spiral stone stairway in search of a late breakfast.

David had been awake and luckily on his own when she entered his room.

Mrs. Livesey had been leaving when Viola arrived, carrying a tray with the remains of a bowl of thin porridge and a plate of thinly cut bread and butter.

She told Viola that David had passed a good night and that his fever was not so intense this morning. He had eaten a little breakfast and, taking everything into account, there were good signs for his eventual recovery.

David had been fretful when Viola insisted that he should not tell anyone here at Glentorran Castle about their amazing change of circumstances in inheriting such a vast fortune from their father.

He could not understand why it was that she was so determined that the Duke did not discover they were now extremely wealthy.

"I don't want to lie to anyone, especially Meg," he insisted, his fingers plucking at the edge of the linen sheet. "I couldn't do that, Viola."

"I wouldn't dream of asking you to lie," she replied firmly, "but perhaps you could just not mention the subject of money at all! You must have hundreds of other things you can talk about with Meg. After all, it isn't at all usual to suddenly tell someone you only know slightly about the state of your family finances!"

David frowned.

He felt so damn weak and ill, but he could tell that this issue really mattered to Viola.

At last he agreed, but wished he could explain to his sister that he did not feel as if this was only the second time he had met Lady Margaret.

He felt he had known her all his life! But he was convinced that Viola would not understand.

Breakfast was served in a small room on the eastern side of the Castle.

The bright morning sun was streaming through the windows and although it made the room seem warmer, it highlighted the worn carpet and threadbare curtains.

It was obvious to Viola that Glentorran Castle did, indeed, need a large amount of money to be spent on it.

The Duke and his sister were drinking coffee and reading the morning's post that had just arrived.

"I trust you find your brother is a little better?" the Duke enquired as Viola slipped into a seat.

"Yes, indeed. I am sure that a few days' rest will see him fully recovered."

Lady Margaret looked up, her eyes intense.

"We must be so careful not to hurry him and cause another relapse," she now counselled. "Doctor Monroe was most precise that David should take things very easily."

Viola shook her head at the maid who was offering her a bowl of porridge and took some fresh bread from a basket in the middle of the table. She then spread a large spoonful of honey on it, enjoying the sweet mouthful.

"It's our own heather honey," the Duke informed her, glancing up from a long and official-looking letter.

His dark eyes gleamed.

"You find it pleasing, Lady Viola?"

She returned his smile.

"Yes, Your Grace. It has a wonderful flavour and fragrance."

The Duke now found himself staring at the sunlight from the window as it played on the gold tendrils of hair that fluttered around her ears in the draught from the half open door.

Pulling himself together, he suggested,

"I was wondering if you would care to be shown a little more of the Glentorran estate this morning? You ride, I am sure."

Viola smiled and nodded her head.

For all their poverty whilst growing up, riding had been one of the country pursuits her father had insisted that she and David learn from an early age.

"Then, if you will forgive me, I will leave you now to finish your breakfast and arrange for a suitable mount to be ready for you. Shall we say at eleven o'clock?"

Viola laughed.

"As long as Lady Margaret can find me something to ride in, I shall be delighted."

"Oh, call me Meg. We did agree remember? Lady Margaret sounds so heavy and old-fashioned!"

The Duke paused as he reached the door and, with a smile, added,

"And I am Robert. That makes life far easier for everyone. I don't hold with all the ceremony and rank that goes with my title."

Lady Margaret smiled at Viola's expression as her brother left the room.

"Robert professes such modern views regarding his title, Viola. He claims a Duke should *earn* the respect he is given, but not expect it as a right."

Viola nodded, realising with some surprise that she agreed with the dark-haired Scottish girl.

"Now if you have finished your breakfast, let's go upstairs and I will find you something to ride in. Thank Heavens we are roughly the same height and shape!"

Just as they were crossing the hall, Mrs. Livesey appeared.

"Oh, Lady Viola, Captain Howard is in the morning room, waiting to speak to you if that is convenient."

"My goodness, yes, I must find out how the other passengers are today. Will you excuse me, Meg?"

"Certainly. I will start sorting out my wardrobe. If you are to be with us for more than a few days, then you will need more than one outfit to wear!"

Viola hurried to the morning room to find Captain Howard standing with his back to the window, his peaked cap in his hands.

"Captain – oh, it is so good to see you fit and well. How are the passengers – Mr. and Mrs. Van Ashton and all the others? We had a message that they were safe, but are they fully recovered from their dreadful ordeal? And what will you do without your beautiful yacht?"

Captain Howard, an elderly American, smiled, his stern grizzled face softening at the sight of this beautiful young English girl, who had been so charming to himself and his crew on their journey across the Atlantic.

"We all survived unscathed, thank you, my Lady. Mr. and Mrs. Van Ashton and the remainder of their party are on their way to London.

"I am heading for Glasgow with my crew. Mr. Van Ashton has to deal with the insurance officials, but assures me he will purchase another motor yacht just as soon as he can. We will wait for his instructions."

Viola clasped her hands together.

"Oh, that is such good news! Now, tell me, was anything salvaged from the wreck?"

Captain Howard frowned.

"A few boxes of cargo, a couple of suitcases, but most was lost."

Viola tried to sound cheerful.

"That is sad, of course, but they are only material possessions. No one has lost their life from that appalling accident, which is the main thing.

"I am writing to my cousin, Miss Matthews, today to tell her what has happened. She is very elderly and I do not wish to alarm her, but it is important that she knows we are safe and well."

The Captain's frown deepened.

He was not sure whether to confide his fears to this lovely girl, but if she was to remain in Scotland, surely she should be warned.

"Lady Viola, have you given any thought as to why the ship ran onto those rocks?"

Viola shook her head, mystified.

"I suppose I imagined it was because of the storm, the wind driving us onto the coast."

"I think that will be the official version, but my men tell me that they steered for the shelter of the shore because they could see a bright light flashing and believed it to be the light showing the way into a harbour."

The dark blue eyes gazing up into his grew even

darker as their owner began to understand exactly what he was implying.

"But surely – no, that cannot be right! – that would mean – "

Captain Howard shook his head grimly.

"Yes, my Lady. It does mean *wreckers*! Dastardly fiends deliberately attempting to entice us poor sailors onto the rocks so they can steal the ship's cargo."

Viola leapt up instantly and walked to the window, gazing out over the tangles of unpruned shrubs and towards the distant mountains.

"I simply cannot believe it. This is 1904, Captain Howard. In this day and age, surely such heinous crimes have long been outlawed."

"Yes, my Lady, but on certain parts of the wilder Cornish coast it still occurs occasionally. I have not heard of it here in Scotland, but my men are quite sure they saw a light."

She could find no words to persuade him otherwise, although privately she was convinced that the lookout had fallen asleep at his post and had not realised how far North the storm had driven the yacht.

She also had a suspicion – because she had heard her father once discussing it with one of his friends – that if human error was discovered to be the cause of the wreck, Mr. Van Ashton would not receive the full amount of any insurance claim.

But what if the Captain was right?

Viola shuddered, feeling suddenly very cold.

That meant that someone on the Glentorran estate had deliberately set out to wreck the boat, not caring who lost their lives in that atrocious sea.

"All I am saying, my Lady, is keep your ears and eyes open while you and his Lordship are here in Scotland.

"Just be on your guard and if you see anything that might confirm my suspicions, let the authorities know of it immediately.

"And now I must take my leave of you. I wish you good day, Lady Viola, and my respects to your brother."

Viola watched the Captain leave.

Deep in thought she made her way upstairs.

She paused outside David's room, wondering if she should tell him what she had just learnt.

But she could hear Meg's voice coming from inside and hesitated.

If she now told Meg, then she would surely inform her brother.

For some strange reason, Viola did not want the Duke to know that there might be a problem on his estate.

She slipped into her own room and smiled as she found riding clothes laid out on her bed.

As she changed, she decided she was worrying over nothing.

'After all,' she said to herself, tying back her long hair with a blue scarf, 'the Captain has just gone through a traumatic experience. He has lost his ship and will surely be blamed. I expect his crew are trying to save him from the authorities – and themselves! Yes, that is what it will be.

'Wreckers, indeed! And in this day and age – what rubbish!'

Viola made her way out of the Castle and through a maze of overgrown pathways round to the stable block.

The Duke was waiting for her, talking to a small thin man whom Viola suspected must be his Head Groom.

Two horses were saddled and ready to ride.

The Duke turned and smiled as the tall slim figure in a dark blue riding skirt and jacket appeared.

"Viola! You look charming. I recognise that outfit, although Meg hardly rides at all these days.

"This is Stuart McAndrew. Stuart used to help his father, Angus, with the gardens and now gives a hand with the few horses that remain here.

"Stuart, this is Lady Viola Northcombe, who, as I am certain you have already heard on the grapevine, was rescued from the sea with her brother, the Earl."

"Mr. McAndrew."

Two bright brown eyes peered at her from beneath bushy eyebrows and a gnarled hand touched an imaginary cap.

"Lady Viola. Glad to see you are none the worse for your misadventure, my Lady."

"Thank you. I am well. It all happened so quickly, there was no time to be scared."

"Aye, these things do happen fast," Stuart replied almost under his breath as Viola was about to ask him what he meant when the Duke broke in,

"Here, let me help you to mount and we will be on our way. Your horse is called Bonnie. She's a nice little mare. We only have three horses left now. My old boy, Brandy here and an old pony that Meg cannot be persuaded to sell. She lets him pull her in a little pony cart down to the village to collect fresh fish when the fleet comes in."

Viola was very aware of the Duke's strength as she put her foot in his cupped hand and let him half-throw her into the saddle.

For a long second his lean tanned fingers lingered on hers as he sorted out the reins and made sure she was comfortable.

He looked up at her and smiled, his dark eyes warm with friendship.

Viola felt hot colour rush into her cheeks.

Why was she feeling so on edge?

The Duke could never mean anything to her.

She watched as he swung himself effortlessly onto his mount and with a brief nod of farewell to the groom, set off down a path that led through the neglected grounds and then away from the Castle and out onto the moors.

Viola glanced around her as she rode, enjoying the sweet breeze that was blowing in from the sea.

She had no difficulty in handling Bonnie and soon urged her into a trot so that where the path widened, she could ride next to the Duke.

"Is this all Glentorran land?"

"Aye, it is."

The Duke shook his head in despair.

"And, as you can see, it is not in good repair. The grounds were immaculate in my grandfather's day. Lawns swept down gracefully from the terrace and there were so many interesting trees and shrubs.

"I must admit that Stuart does seem a little on the elderly side to be gardening full time," remarked Viola, not wishing to sound critical.

The Duke laughed, but it was not a happy sound.

"You should meet his father! Old Angus. He was the Head Gardener for years at Glentorran. He has a little croft up on the moors, but he refuses to leave his cottage in the Castle grounds."

The track was leading them upwards now, winding its way through great sheets of heather.

Somewhere overhead a lark was singing about the glorious day and bees were busy everywhere.

"I should have thought it would be marvellous to live up here amongst all this magnificent scenery."

The Duke smiled across at the beautiful girl, whose hair had pulled free from the blue scarf and was blowing in pale blonde tendrils across her cheeks.

"Magnificent now, that is true, but in the winter the snow comes down from the mountains and these moors are cold and bleak. Still beautiful but deadly as well."

"Oh! I can see sheep on the mountainside."

The Duke nodded and pointed with his whip.

"You are right. The estate earns most of its income from sheep – from their wool. Luckily for the sheep, their lifestyle does not make them good to eat! All that running about across the moors makes the meat tough.

"If you stay in Glentorran for long, you are sure to meet some of the shepherds. They are a law to themselves but good men."

Viola hesitated to make any remark that could give offence, but her honesty at last forced her to say,

"Although, of course, it is none of my business, I have heard that Glentorran has fallen a little on hard times recently."

The Duke did not reply immediately.

He was busy keeping Brandy in check. The horse had spooked as a rabbit took off from almost under his hooves.

At last he replied,

"I am sure it is quite obvious to someone who is in the same position. All the signs are here. The lack of staff, the plainness of the food, how incredibly shabby the Castle has become and as for the grounds –

"Yes, Viola, you and your brother, more than most people will, I am sure, understand the plight of Glentorran.

"My father – well, I will not speak ill of the dead! Let me just say that there were debts that had to be settled when I inherited the title, some of which I am still paying!"

"My father – "

Viola paused and then continued slowly,

"My father was a man who chased after dreams all his life. And chasing dreams costs money. David and I never went hungry or cold, but our lives could have been very much easier if Papa had stayed at home."

The Duke sighed.

"I could even accept the situation with more grace if my father had had dreams of making Glentorran a better place – a *Castle of Dreams*. But he hardly ever came up to Scotland. His time was spent gambling in London.

"And it isn't just the Castle that has been neglected. The people who live in the surrounding areas have such a hard life.

"Do you know there is not a hospital for over a hundred miles? My people here often die before they can be treated. Our one doctor does his very best, but the poor cannot pay him and fish or vegetables do not help him that much!

"If I had sufficient money, I would build a hospital somewhere close by. A place where operations could be performed, broken bones set and lives saved."

And without another word he urged his horse into a canter and Viola's mount followed.

Together they crested a steep rise and reined in to gaze down on the coastline that lay before them.

The sea this morning was like pale blue silk, hardly breaking over the rocky reef that ran parallel to the beach. It was hard to believe that this was the very same sea that had so pounded and destroyed the Van Ashton's beautiful yacht.

The Duke pointed with his whip again.

"Over there, do you see the manse and the houses surrounding it, Viola? Follow along a way and you will see the harbour where the fishing fleet is moored. That is all part of the Glentorran estate."

"Oh, was it those boats who so bravely rescued us all yesterday?"

"Aye, that it was."

"May I be allowed to thank them?"

The Duke smiled.

"Certainly. Although they would not expect to be thanked for performing such a service. They are all most independent characters, these people of our fishing village. But we can make our way down there by all means."

Side by side they rode down the track towards the harbour.

"Who was the man who so expertly rowed David and me to shore?" enquired Viola.

He laughed.

"Oh, that was Fergus – Fergus Lyall. I have known him all my life. You see, when I was a bairn, I lived with my parents and wee Meg in Edinburgh. But City life did not suit me and I was often sent up here to Glentorran to stay with my grandfather.

"He was very elderly and he loved the quiet of the library. Poor man, I was a wild rowdy boy who must have tried his patience to the limit! I lived outdoors most of the time and soon found friends in the fishing village. Fergus and I grew up together, until I was sent to boarding school, of course."

Viola could picture him in her mind.

A small dark-haired boy in an old kilt and probably a dirty torn jersey, running through the long heather with a dog panting at his heels, full of the high spirits of youth, never dreaming of what lay ahead of him.

The track to the village grew stonier and cut deeply between two sides of the cliff face.

Viola needed all her horsemanship skills to keep in the saddle as Bonnie slid and slithered down the slope, her hooves sending up little sparks from the cobbles.

At last they reached the harbour, a small half-circle cut into the coastline as if it was a bite taken from a piece of bread.

A stone jetty ran out to the entrance of the harbour with all the Glentorran fishing fleet moored alongside, their paintwork gleaming red and blue, emerald and black.

Overhead seagulls screamed and dived for small tit-bits as one of the boats had just landed its catch.

Some of the women, shawls draped over their heads, were sorting out fish from crabs.

"I love all the different colours of the boats," Viola enthused.

"Every family traditionally owns a different colour. Never tell anyone, but I have a preference for the scarlet ones, but Fergus owns that dark blue vessel, moored right at the far end. His father taught us both to sail when we were just lads."

Viola admired the fleet, wondering how odd it must have felt for the Duke when he realised that he would grow up to inherit the Glentorran estate whilst his friend would stay a fisherman.

"You have remained friends?" she asked hesitantly, trying to understand.

The Duke chuckled.

"Dear Lord, yes. Here in Scotland the people have a different approach to titles, Viola. I may be the Duke of

Glentorran but as far as Fergus is concerned, I am still Rob, the boy who cannot swim as far and fast as he can.

"I am also Godfather to his own lad, Ian. We had hoped our boys would grow up together, too, but – "

He stopped, his face darkening.

"Well, never mind all of that. Come and meet him and his wife, Heather. I am certain they will be delighted to see you."

The two riders trotted through the village and Viola noticed that the men and women acknowledged the Duke, but there was no servility in their bearing.

She was very impressed – she had visited too many estates where the staff and tenants seemed almost in fear of their Master and landlord.

The end of a long line of terraced cottages was the Duke's destination.

As they reined to a halt outside, Viola was full of admiration for the glowing window boxes full of flowers.

"Fergus! Heather! Ahoy inside."

The dark blue door opened and the redheaded man strode out, who she had last seen rowing her and David to safety through the storm.

A wide smile creased his tanned face.

The Duke dismounted, tossed the reins over a post and then helped Viola down.

"Fergus, let me introduce Lady Viola Northcombe. Viola, this is Fergus Lyall."

"Thank you so much for rescuing us!" cried Viola, shaking the hard hand held out to her. "You were *so* brave, Fergus, to tackle that raging sea."

"Och, think nothing of it, my Lady. I was only too happy to help out. Heather! Come quickly, lass, the Duke and a guest are here. Do forgive my wife, my Lady. She is just putting our wee boy down to sleep."

The door of the cottage opened again and a fresh complexioned, pretty young woman with bright brown hair came out, a shawl pinned closely round her shoulders.

Viola held out her hand and then was hardly aware of the introductions being made.

She could not take her eyes away from the brooch that was pinning the Scottish girl's shawl.

Large and ornate, it glittered in the spring sunshine.

To some it would have appeared to be just a piece of paste of no great value.

But Viola knew better.

The very last time she had seen this huge cluster of diamonds, it had been pinned prominently on the front of Mrs. Van Ashton's evening gown!

CHAPTER FIVE

Lady Margaret ran up the circular stone stairway leading from the Great Hall of the Castle, hurried along the corridor and knocked on David's door.

"Come in, Meg!"

She entered the room and smiled in surprise at the sight of David sitting in a large chair by the open window.

He was still looking somewhat thin and pale, but his eyes were bright and he was smiling cheerfully.

"How did you know it was me?"

David's smile deepened.

"Everyone taps on the door in a different way. My sister raps on it with two sharp knocks, Mrs. Livesey and the maids are very tentative. Your brother gives three equal taps and yours, Meg – "

"Yes?"

"Yours are a series of little noises. As if a small bird was asking to be let in!"

Meg chuckled.

"What utter nonsense you talk! Obviously, David, you are feeling much better?"

David patted the wide casement seat opposite him and Meg sat down, smoothing the creases from her green skirt and wishing that it did no look quite so shabby in the bright sunlight that flooded into the room.

"Yes, indeed. Thanks to you and all the wonderful

care your staff have given me, I hope to venture downstairs tomorrow. I would have liked to have joined you for dinner tonight, but Mrs. Livesey just turned several shades of puce when I mentioned it!"

"Dear Dorcas Livesey. I have known her all my life. I admit I used to be scared of her when I was small, but I know better now. She seems such a dragon, but under that stern exterior beats a very soft heart."

David nodded.

"She has been kindness itself to me and I think my recovery would have been very slow without her nursing skills. Although I seem to have eaten more porridge in the last couple of days than ever before in my whole life!"

Lady Margaret gazed through the open window.

The room looked out towards the distant mountains, majestic and covered with heather and, unconsciously, she sighed at the sight of them.

David frowned.

"You do not seem your usual cheerful self, Meg. Is there a problem? Is it causing difficulties, my sister and I being here in the Castle?"

She turned to him, her great dark eyes anxious.

"No, no! Please, never think that! I am delighted you are both here. You have no idea how wonderful it is, David, to talk to someone of my own age who has visited foreign countries, travelled across the sea and seen things I will never see."

"I have only travelled to America and once there I stayed in New York. I never got to see Niagara Falls or the Grand Canyon or any of the other wonderful sights. And all I saw of the voyage home was the inside of my cabin! Admittedly, I long to journey around the world, but – "

"Like me, you do not have enough money for such

a trip!" Lady Margaret interrupted. "Oh, I know exactly how you feel. Sometimes when I look out at the mountains and instead of seeing their beauty, I see them all as a line of gaolers, keeping me here in this Castle prison!"

David scowled to himself.

How easy it would be to say that he had plenty of money now. That he could afford to go round the world twice and not notice the difference to his bank balance.

But he made a promise to Viola that he would keep quiet about the fortune they had inherited from their father.

Now he was wishing with all his heart that he had not made such a commitment to his sister.

"Do you feel so very isolated here in Glentorran?" he asked quietly.

She played with a piece of thread that was hanging from the worn edge of her sleeve.

"Oh, please don't get the wrong impression, David! I love my brother and Glentorran. But – I *long* to travel!

"I have been to Glasgow, Edinburgh and London. Three big cities. But I don't like busy places. I want to see deserts and oceans and the vast open plains of Africa! And I know that I never will.

"There is a whole exciting and different world out there and I am passionate to experience it all."

David reached over and caught her hands in his.

He snapped off the loose thread and twined it round his finger.

"I sympathise, Meg. I really do. Viola has always wanted to live in England, to have a house in the country and create a wonderful garden. She loves dogs and horses and all sorts of country pursuits.

"But, although we are twins, I am not that keen on the energetic outdoor life she likes so much. Just give me a sketchbook, a small box of watercolours and a marvellous view and I will be a happy man.

"But most of all, I, too, would like to travel. I think I am very like my father in that desire. He could never stay in one place for long.

"I, just like you, ache to see the Arabian deserts, the Sahara, the jungles of Borneo and the unusual animals and beautiful flowers of the South Sea Islands."

"Robert told me a little about your family history," sighed Lady Margaret. "All four of us are victims of our fathers' careless behaviour, so it seems."

David did not reply.

He twined the thread even tighter, hardly noticing the pain on his skin.

How could he agree with this wonderful girl?

What she had said would have been true a year ago when they had first met at Charlotte Brent's birthday ball in London.

Then he had just been David, the Viscount Powell, without a care in the world or a penny to his name.

But now he was the Earl of Northcombe, the *very rich* Earl of Northcombe!

He now owned oil fields and all sorts of companies in the United States. He had to instruct his partner, Lewis Wilder, and discharge his many responsibilities.

Once he was fully recovered and they were back in London, he knew he would have to plunge into a world of finance that he knew nothing about and cared nothing for.

"Perhaps things will change one day?" he ventured, but she just laughed.

"Aye, perhaps we will all come into a fortune! An old gypsy woman came into the Castle last Christmas and told me I would marry a very rich man. I asked her where he was, but all she would say was that he lived across the water! But, as far as I know, there are no such candidates living in the Hebrides seeking my hand in marriage!"

David chuckled.

"And what did she tell your brother?"

Lady Margaret's laugh rang out again.

"Och, Robert was most put out. She told him he would have his heart broken by a man from over the seas! As Robert said, he wouldn't mind if it was a woman who broke his heart, but he could not see himself getting that upset by anything a man told him!"

David decided to change the subject.

"Tell me, Meg. I noticed that Viola was strangely quiet this morning when she came to visit me. It was most unlike her.

"I asked her if she had enjoyed her ride with your brother yesterday and she assured me that she indeed had. Did you notice anything untoward regarding her behaviour at dinner last night?"

Meg looked concerned.

"Now you mention it, your sister did indeed seem a little quiet. Almost as if she had something on her mind that was worrying her.

"Robert was called out during the meal – a problem somewhere on the estate needed his immediate attention. Viola refused coffee and retired early. Perhaps it is just a reaction to the last few hectic days. After all, David, you were both shipwrecked only the other day!"

The young Earl laughed and agreed with her, but he could not get his twin's serious face out of his mind.

They had always been very close and he knew that something had upset his sister and wondered if she would tell him about it.

In the meantime he could only hope that it would not cause any problems during the remainder of their stay here at Glentorran Castle.

*

Viola had breakfasted in her room and once she had finished, she pulled on the warm tweed jacket that Meg had provided for her, paid a brief visit to David to check on his progress and then hurried outside into the rambling Castle grounds.

There had been no sign of the Duke or his sister at breakfast, but a maid she met as she crossed the Great Hall informed her that the Duke had been away from home by six o'clock that morning.

It was a fine warm day and the air tasted like wine. A light breeze was blowing in from the sea and little clouds scudded overhead.

Viola had hardly slept all night.

She had tossed and turned restlessly, seeing in front of her eyes the diamond brooch pinned to Heather Lyall's shawl – the brooch that had belonged to Mrs. Van Ashton who had worn it so often on their trip across the Atlantic.

'There is no way that piece of jewellery could have survived the shipwreck,' Viola murmured to herself as she wandered through the overgrown shrubberies.

'Even if Mrs. Van Ashton had been wearing it – and I am certain she was not – then it would have sunk to the floor of the ocean if it fell from her bodice.

'One of the fishermen must have taken it from the wreck. But why would they give it to Fergus? Is he their chief? And if that is so, was he behind the ship's tragic end? Is Captain Howard right? Were wreckers the cause of the yacht smashing into the rocks?'

She then caught her hand on a bunch of nettles and grunted.

Apparently dangers were lurking even in this quiet deserted garden!

'But Fergus is the Duke's special boyhood friend! So how could I possibly accuse him of such treachery?' her thoughts ran on miserably.

She was just beginning to realise that her feelings for the Duke were growing day by day.

Although she could see no future for them because of the horrid way fate had turned her from a poor girl into a very rich one, she knew that hurting him was something she could never do.

And she recognised by the light-hearted way he had spoken to Fergus and Heather Lyall and by the way he had asked after their little boy, his Godson, that these fisherfolk meant a great deal to him.

She could sense that the Duke would only ever give his trust sparingly.

He had given it to the Lyalls.

How could she be the one to spoil all that for him?

Still deep in thought, she turned a corner and then stopped and gasped.

In front of her was a flight of stone steps, leading down into a square walled rose garden.

Everywhere she looked roses grew in wild abandon with great swathes of pink, yellow and red cascading over the old bricks.

Tall standard varieties studded with crimson, white and apricot flowers, bushes of old roses covered in smaller bunches of white tinged with pink and yellow blushing into pink and a red so dark it was almost black.

And on the air floated the most incredible perfume.

Viola could hardly believe her senses.

She ran down the rough stone steps and cupped the nearest rose to inhale the wonderful smell.

"You like yon flower, then, lassie?"

Viola spun round.

A very elderly man was standing watching her. He was wearing old corduroy breeches and heavy boots. His hair was sparse and white and he leant on a gnarled stick.

"These roses have the most amazing smell! I have never seen such a wonderful rose garden. I thought you would have difficulty in growing such fine specimens this far North."

"Angus will tell you he can grow roses anywhere!"

Viola turned round, startled.

The Duke was standing on the stone steps, gazing down at her, his dark hair tousled by the summer breeze.

"Your Grace," the old man wheezed and raised a knuckle to his lined forehead.

"Pay no attention to Angus McAndrew's courtesy to me, Viola," the Duke added. "He has been a gardener here at Glentorran since my grandfather's day.

"He taught me how to fish, how to shoot and how to ride a horse. He even larruped my backside once when Fergus and I accidentally smashed a window in one of his glasshouses!"

The old man's eyes gleamed under his bushy white brows.

"That young red-headed devil was always up to no good, Your Grace, and dragging you with him, as I recall. And you got the punishment, because he ran off and you couldna do so!"

The Duke chuckled.

"Viola, this is Angus McAndrew. You met his son,

Stuart, yesterday. Angus, this is Lady Viola Northcombe. She and her brother – "

"Aye, shipwrecked they were indeed, so I've been told. Weel, you're a bonny lass, that's for sure, my Lady. And you like the rose there, I see."

Viola was holding up a white rose, its petals tinged with pink, so perfect she could almost have cried.

"It is wonderful. How do you grow them like this in such a harsh climate, Mr. McAndrew?"

"Angus has green fingers – and is helped a lot by the Gulf Stream!" the Duke told her. "It brings warm air and warm waters to this coastline. Our temperature is far less severe than other parts of Scotland."

He reached over and snapped off a bloom.

Angus handed the Duke a long knife and he swiftly stripped away the thorns and threaded the stem through the buttonhole of Viola's jacket.

"This particular rose is called '*Grace Darling*'," he murmured and Viola could feel the colour flush up into her cheeks as his fingers brushed against her neck.

"Thank you! It is lovely," she managed to whisper, deciding that it was just her imagination that had made her think he had paused briefly between the words *Grace* and *Darling*!

Angus took back his knife, glanced towards Viola and then said something in a strange language to the Duke before hobbling out of the rose garden, chuckling under his breath.

"What on earth did he say?" Viola asked the Duke, desperately searching for a safe subject. "It sounded very weird."

"That was in Gaelic, the language of the Highlands. You will often hear it spoken around Glentorran. Now, let me escort you back to the Castle. I am sure you will be glad of a cool drink after your walk."

He offered Viola his arm which she now accepted gratefully, but was well aware as they left the rose garden that he had not told her what remark the old gardener had made about her.

The Duke held back a long branch that swept down from a bush across the overgrown path.

"Men like Angus McAndrew and his son are the life-blood of Glentorran," he told her. "They have worked, man and boy for the estate all their lives.

"I have no idea how old Angus is, but his father and his father before him worked for the Glentorrans. And that is the same for almost every family for miles around.

"So I am sure you can imagine how hard it is for me to even consider for a moment giving up the estate and leaving them to their fate. But I would expect your family will have similar problems."

He laughed unhappily, as he added,

"Money may well be the root of all evil, but I could do a lot of good with just a little!"

Viola cast a swift glance up at his troubled face.

She could hear the passion and despair in his voice and longed to speak out – to tell him that she was no longer poor.

She recognised she was living in his home under false pretences.

It would only take her a second to tell him – but she hesitated, because in that short time, she realised she would lose his friendship for ever.

How he would despise a girl who pretended to be poor when she was not. He would see her as someone who had no moral fibre and no idea of what was decent, right or wrong.

"In America I learnt that they are trying to do away with the idea that one man should have the well-being of a whole district in his hands," she ventured.

The Duke shouldered his way between two overgrown shrubs and Viola followed behind him, unaware that a cascade of white blossom had fallen on her golden hair.

He turned round and almost exclaimed out loud at how beautiful she looked.

For a second he felt compelled to tell her and then with a strong physical effort, he schooled his expression to remain calm.

There was no way he could have a future with Lady Viola Northcombe.

He had nothing to offer her – only a life of poverty, and he was quite sure she had already experienced enough of that.

No, he was sure that Viola would soon meet some rich titled fellow who would whisk her away to his home and he, Robert, would never see her again.

He forced himself to remember what she had been talking about.

"Yes, there is a lot to be said for making my tenants more self-reliant. And the fishermen are, of course. They can feed their families and sell their catch at market. They will not suffer if Glentorran has to be sold.

"But there are hundreds of others on the estate who will find their world a colder and more difficult place if I am forced to give up the Castle."

He tried to sound cheerful.

"Och, this is a dreary subject for so fine a day! Don't you worry about my problems, Viola. I will be away to London again soon. I am sure my bankers will find me someone who is keen to invest in an impoverished Scottish Dukedom!"

Viola turned to him.

She could bear this no longer!

She would tell him the truth about her father, the oil fields and the vast sums of money that she and David had inherited on his death.

She would now suggest that the Northcombe family should invest into the Glentorran estate and that between them they would make a big difference.

She took a deep breath.

"Robert – " she began.

At that precise moment the Duke turned abruptly away from Viola –

"Look over there! Here is Meg come to find us, no doubt. Hello, my little sister. Am I neglecting my duties in some way? That frown on your face does not spell good news, I am sure."

Lady Margaret reached up and kissed his cheek.

"Only Mr. Campbell from town, Robert. Worrying about his bill for cattle feed once more!

"I have asked him to wait in the library and said I would come to find you immediately. But if we walk very slowly, he might have lost patience and left!"

The Duke sighed heavily and the mournful sound tore at Viola's heart.

Viola could tell just how greatly he cared about his inheritance and all the responsibilities it carried.

How difficult he really must find it, to have to beg a tradesman for time to pay a bill.

She fell silent as they made their way slowly back to the Castle.

Her chance to set things straight between them had disappeared for now, but she would have to find a way of speaking to the Duke again very soon.

Because there was also the problem of Fergus and the diamond brooch!

Viola groaned inwardly.

Goodness, how complicated her life had become in such a short time!

CHAPTER SIX

The following day dawned sparkling and clear over Glentorran Castle, the distant mountains sharply etched in purple against a pale blue sky.

The sea was lapping quietly against the shore and it was impossible to believe that it could ever be wild enough to sink a ship and put lives at risk.

The local people would have told Viola and David that these signs were deceptive, that there was a great deal of bad weather to come later that day, but at the moment it was warm and fine.

Viola had spent a restless night tossing and turning, worrying about how soon an opportunity would arise when she could tell the Duke she was no longer poor like him, but together with David was the owner of a vast fortune.

Unable to sleep she climbed out of bed and gazed out of her window at the moonlit landscape.

She decided that after dinner that evening would be the best time for the face to face she dreaded so much.

She would ask for a private word with the Duke in his study and confess to him that she had kept the change in her circumstances secret.

'And I can easily guess what his reaction will be!' she murmured wryly to herself, leaning out of the casement window to breathe in the fresh night air.

'Indeed, I cannot blame him. How would I react if our roles were reversed? I would feel all my trust had been betrayed!'

But Viola still felt a little better for having made up her mind to take a specific course of action and returning to bed finally fell asleep.

After breakfast she was surprised to see a sea mist rolling in, hiding the high mountains from view and filling the air with a fine drizzle.

Walking in the grounds was not an option, so Viola decided to make some alterations to the rest of the clothes Lady Margaret had found for her to wear.

She was wearying of always dining in the same old plain blouse and skirt. There was a pretty primrose dress with a becoming high collar and long sleeves edged in lace that would fit her with a few small adjustments.

The Duke had not appeared at breakfast – no doubt he had left the Castle very early once again.

Viola was working in the small drawing room, the primrose dress lying across her lap in a shimmery tangle as she was studying it, when the door opened and her brother limped slowly in, his grey eyes smiling.

He was wearing an ancient Glentorran kilt and she clapped her hands in glee at the sight.

"David! How wonderful. You are well enough to come downstairs. Are you sure? You do not wish to over-tax your strength. And I am sure that putting on a kilt must have taken a lot of your energy! If your friends in London and New York could only see you now!"

The young Earl walked over to a chair next to Viola and sank into it with a slight moan.

"Goodness me, those stairs were steeper than I had thought! You can mock me, Viola, but the kilt is strangely comfortable and although I could wish for my legs to be a little bit stronger, I don't think I would shame this garment too much!

"And yes, I am well on the road to recovery, Viola. Indeed, I think if I can continue to progress at this rate, we could make plans to leave at the end of the week."

"*Leave*?"

Viola could not prevent a cold wave of unhappiness sweeping over her.

David sighed.

"I know just how you feel. I, too, am loath to say goodbye to Glentorran. But life goes on, Sis. We must get back to London and pick up the threads of our own world.

"And I am sure that Robert and Meg, as hospitable as they are, will be glad to have their home to themselves once more. We must be a drain on their slender resources.

"But – " he now hesitated, looking very young and uneasy – "before we go, I want you to release me from my promise. I need to tell Meg of our change in circumstances. I cannot leave her believing the lie that I am as poor as she and her brother."

Viola bent her golden head over the silk dress, tears threatening to fall.

Her twin brother was not the only one who needed to confess.

"David, I really must tell the Duke first. It is only polite. Please give me until tomorrow night and I promise you that I will explain the situation to him before then."

David looked closely at his sister's beautiful face.

They often thought alike and he was certain that he understood how she was feeling.

"You like the Duke? More than like him, perhaps?"

Viola flushed and tossed her head.

She now turned away to gaze out of the window, not wanting her brother to see the pain in her eyes.

"What nonsense you do talk, David! Of course, I like the Duke. Robert is a fine man, but I hardly know him or he me. We are just – friends – acquaintances. I am just a guest who he has been forced to shelter. I am sure that as soon as we leave Scotland, he will not give me a second thought."

David was about to begin arguing with her, when Lady Margaret appeared in the doorway.

She hesitated, aware of an atmosphere in the room.

"I am so sorry," she started to say, "I do hope I am not interrupting, but oh, David, it is so good to see you up and about once more. And wearing such a bonny kilt! I am very impressed."

David stood up, all his earlier tiredness apparently forgotten.

"Meg – good morning! And yes, as you can see, I am becoming stronger with every passing minute and I am hoping that you will take my arm and show me some of the Castle grounds.

"Look, your good housekeeper, Mrs. Livesey, has found an old sketchbook for me. I have promised to be very careful with it because some of the pages have already been used. But if you can find me a good place to sit, I plan to draw to record my own memories of your beautiful home."

Lady Margaret's eyes shone and her cheeks burnt pink.

"I would be so delighted to help you. The rain has vanished as quickly as it came and the sun is shining once more to welcome you outside."

David walked across the room to stand beside her and then turned back to Viola, his face grave.

"I shall abide, of course, by your wishes, Viola, but only until tomorrow."

And then they were both gone and Viola could only sit still, fighting back the tears that threatened to overcome her once more.

Meg and David walked slowly out of the Castle and down the steps into the wild garden.

A quick glance at David's white face told Meg that he was not as strong as he thought and she made an excuse to sit on a stone bench, gazing out across the cliff-tops to where the sea met the sky in a dark blue line.

"I wish I had a boat and could sail away – " David said at last, opening the sketchbook and reaching for one of the many pencils Mrs. Livesey had found for him.

"To foreign lands?"

"Yes, indeed! And to see all those exotic places I dream of. But there is no good in dreaming. Instead I have to travel down to London at the end of the week!"

Meg took a deep breath.

She knew something was bothering him, but would it be very forward to ask?

Surely they were good enough friends for him to be honest with her.

"Sometimes you seem so troubled about the future, David – " she began.

Suddenly he put down his pencil and reached out to take her hand.

Meg gave a little gasp, but did not pull away.

"Meg, will you trust me? It is so very true, there is something most important I have to tell you, but I have promised Viola that – "

She interrupted swiftly, an expression of irritation crossing her usually calm face.

"David, do you always have to do what your sister

requests? Sometimes it appears to me that she seems to control your life."

The young Earl shook his head.

"That just isn't true. I agree that because of the odd way we have been brought up, we are very close and often like to do the same things, but in many other ways we are completely different.

"But on this occasion, my silence is because I made a promise and until I am released from it, I am, of course, honour bound not to speak.

"Come to this bench tomorrow morning, if you still wish to know and then I shall tell you everything!"

Meg felt her cheeks redden.

She knew so little of the real world and even less of men. Should she give him any encouragement? She had no idea what her brother would think of her behaviour.

She glanced at his hand holding hers and gasped.

Still entwined around his little finger was the cotton thread David had cut from her sleeve the day before!

Meg looked at him gravely, but a smile glimmered deep in her dark eyes.

"If you have a wife and children living in London, then I think it would be somewhat courteous if you told me *now*! Otherwise, yes, I will wait until tomorrow, David."

And she sat quietly, watching as his clever fingers sped over the page, sketching the scene he saw before him and dreaming all the time of tropical lands where brightly-coloured parrots flew in the sky instead of the seagulls that spiralled above the cliffs of Glentorran.

*

Back at the Castle, Viola had finished altering the primrose dress and wondered how to spend the rest of the morning.

She gazed wistfully out of the window, wondering about walking down to the beach.

The tide was out and she was keen to explore.

Then she smiled.

In the distance she could see David and Meg sitting side by side on a bench.

She decided to stay inside the Castle as she did not want to venture out in case she met up with them!

She felt a third party would be one too many in that situation.

It seemed odd to see her brother so comfortable in a young woman's presence.

He was not a man who made friends easily, much preferring his painting and sketching hobbies.

But Lady Margaret Glentorran had certainly found a way past his usual reserve.

'But what hope is there for such a union?'

Viola was whispering to herself as she roamed the stone passageways of Glentorran Castle.

'I fear that Meg has as much pride as her brother. She will be worried that people will think she likes David just because he is now extremely rich.'

She found herself at the end of a straight corridor on the second floor of the tall tower at the North side of the castle.

She pushed open a door and cried out in delight.

A large music room lay before her and although the carpet and curtains were old and shabby, the grand piano in the middle of the room shone from regular polishing and when Viola touched one of the keys it sounded in tune.

She sat on the tartan covered piano stool and played a little lullaby she had learnt a long time ago.

"You have a good touch, Viola."

She spun round –

The Duke of Glentorran had been sitting in a high-backed armchair on the far side of the room hidden from her view.

Now he stood up, a sheaf of papers in his hand, his dark hair tousled.

"Oh, you startled me! I am so sorry. Did I disturb you? I thought this room was empty."

"No need to apologise. I am only too pleased to be diverted from reading these lists of figures over and over again. They are poor fare for such a lovely day."

He smiled at Viola, his serious face suddenly alight with warmth.

"The piano belongs to Meg by the way and not me. She plays it very well, but she is so busy these days trying to cope with everything in the Castle with so few staff that she has no time to practise."

He stood up, crossed to the piano and stood looking down at Viola.

"I confess I am surprised to find you indoors, Viola. I just imagined that you would be out in our wild gardens or walking on the beach."

Viola blushed.

There was no way she could tell him she had been trying not to disturb her brother and his sister!

"I intend to go for a walk soon," she murmured. "I want to explore the Castle this morning. I have only seen a little of it so far and I would hate to leave Scotland without knowing all its beauty and surprises."

He laughed, his normally stern face transformed.

"Och, Viola, I think you could explore Glentorran Castle for months and still not discover all its secrets.

"Why, only recently I was searching for a book up in the attic and discovered a cupboard full of old paintings. Obviously they had been stored away many years ago and forgotten."

"And do you like them?"

The Duke smiled.

"It's very hard to tell. They are so dirty and dusty. I imagine that they must have been collected by one of my ancestors. I must show them to your brother one evening. Perhaps he can tell me how old they are."

Viola turned away from him so he could not see her face.

"So the Castle has its own mysteries. What about you? Do you have any secrets, Robert?"

"Me?"

The Duke sounded surprised.

"No, I do not believe in secrets. They only cause trouble and grief."

"But sometimes people will keep information and opinions from their friends and family because they might upset them or be hurtful in some way."

The Duke shook his head.

"No, Viola. I agree that at times people do things out of a misguided sense of caring. But I have no time for such actions. Tell the truth and shame the devil – that is my motto and always will be."

Viola now stood up abruptly, her fingers hitting the keyboard with a loud harsh noise.

She winced.

"If you will excuse me, I must get myself ready for lunch and go for my walk," she blurted out as she hurried towards the door.

The Duke stared after her frowning.

Whatever had he said to upset her, as her mood had certainly changed in the last few minutes.

"Before you leave me – I meant to ask you, Viola. Tonight the fisherfolk are holding a ceilidh in Glentorran village. I am just wondering if you would be interested in attending?"

Viola turned to look at him.

"A ceilidh?"

Robert smiled.

"An evening of Scottish songs and dancing. It will not be like any dance you have ever attended before! The music will be loud and exciting, but I am certain you will enjoy it.

"I would, of course, ask your brother as well, but Meg tells me that he is not strong enough yet for a night of such wild entertainment and she has agreed to stay behind and keep him company."

"Do you always attend the village affairs?"

"Well, I consider it is my duty to show an interest in everything that happens on the Glentorran estate, but, to tell the truth, I would go anyway!"

He laughed.

"I used to love going to the ceilidhs when I was a young boy. Staying here with my grandfather for weeks at a time was enjoyable, but there was never much chance of excitement. Our evenings would be often spent with him reading to me or relating lurid tales of wicked ancestors and what my duties would be when I inherited the estate."

"Heavy fare for a small boy," said Viola gently, her blue eyes sympathetic.

"Indeed! Except that I always enjoyed the tales of the bad ancestors!"

The Duke's dark eyes gleamed.

"My grandfather's youngest brother was banished abroad because his behaviour was so scandalous!

"But those talks didn't take up too many hours. As you can so easily imagine, when I could, I escaped to the fishing village to spend time with my friend Fergus.

"The many nights when the villagers held a ceilidh are still clear in my memory. We used to sit on the floor and wonder at the flying feet, drinking in all the noise, the colour and the excitement.

"Of course, as I grew up, I was taught the Scottish dances. They are very different from the sedate affairs you have attended in London!"

He smiled at Viola and her heart turned over at the warmth in his eyes.

"I would like you to experience a ceilidh before you leave Scotland. The dances are extremely easy. Strip the Willow, the Gay Gordons and the Eightsome Reel. And, if we are very lucky, the men might perform a sword dance for us."

Viola hesitated.

She knew that she should refuse.

Every time she was in the Duke's company and did not confess to the fortune she and David now possessed, she was making the whole situation worse.

And she still had not decided what to do about the thorny problem of the brooch she was sure his friend had stolen from the wreckage of the ship.

Captain Howard had been so certain that there were wreckers at work on this Scottish coastline.

And Fergus could well be the ringleader.

How could she possibly get involved in uncovering such an appalling plot when it was one of Robert's friends involved?

Although how could she stand back and perhaps let it happen again?

But oh, it would be wonderful to spend the evening with the Duke, to see another little glimpse of the world he loved so much, a world she was now beginning to realise was one she, too, could happily live in.

But, after tonight, she knew that she would tell him the truth and their friendship would abruptly end.

But she wanted this one last memory to treasure for the rest of her life – she and the Duke dancing together as they had done that faraway night in London.

"If you think my presence would be welcome – " she began.

The Duke broke in swiftly.

"I know my people will be only too delighted if you are there."

He held out his hand.

"*As would I!*"

A shiver of sheer delight ran through Viola's body and she reached out to briefly place her hand in his.

The warm strong fingers closed around hers for a few seconds, but in that brief time, Viola knew that she had lost her heart for ever.

She was falling in love with Robert, the Duke of Glentorran!

A gentleman of honour who seemed to like her.

But even as their hands dropped apart, Viola knew that this love was doomed.

As soon as the Duke was told the whole truth, he would despise her and long for the day when she and her brother would leave his home.

CHAPTER SEVEN

By eight o'clock that evening, the clouds had rolled in from the mountains, covering the moon and stars.

Viola could smell rain in the air as she made her way slowly down the stone steps from the Great Hall of the Castle to where the Duke was waiting for her.

He looked incredibly distinguished in his heavy kilt and dark green jacket, the buckles on his shoes gleaming, the ruffles on his white shirt ironed to perfection.

He held out his hand to Viola and smiled, his dark eyes softening as she approached.

"You look wonderful! I was wondering what you would wear. I had forgotten that dress of Meg's."

Viola laughed a little nervously.

The lovely white dress with a plaid draped across one shoulder was a little tight on her and she realised that every inch of her figure was now outlined by the soft white material.

"It is so very beautiful. The most beautiful dress I have ever worn!"

The Duke shook his head.

"No, that would undoubtedly be the blue gown you were wearing that evening so long ago now at Charlotte Brent's ball. You looked just like an ice Princess."

"That sounds very chilly!"

"Just – untouchable!" came the swift reply.

Viola was aware of the hot colour flooding up into her cheeks and turned her attention to the little pony cart.

Stuart McAndrew was standing holding the bridle of a fat grey pony who peered round curiously as if to see what the delay was all about.

"Is this our transport for the ceilidh?" Viola asked with a smile.

"Aye. It is a little far to walk – going down to the village is fine, but coming back here late at night could be wearying. You will be tired from dancing, I expect."

The Duke patted the grey pony.

"Bolster will trundle us down slowly to Glentorran with perfect ease, as long as he is allowed to walk at his own pace!"

The Duke helped Viola into the cart, sprang up to sit next to her, took the reins from the groom and slapped them against the broad grey back in front of him.

Bolster hesitated for a second and then reluctantly ambled forward.

Viola jolted sharply sideways as the wheels rocked over the cobbled pathway and the Duke's arm shot out to encircle her shoulders, holding her fast against his side as the little cart made its way down the steep slope towards the fishing village.

She gave a little sigh of sheer contentment and, for a brief moment, allowed her head to just touch the Duke's shoulder.

She could not remember when she had last been so happy and at the same time so fearful of losing all she held so dear.

Bolster walked very slowly, but it was still far too fast for Viola.

Eventually the little cart reached the village just as it

began to pour with rain and the Duke guided them to the doorway of a barn close to the last few cottages.

A small boy appeared and ran out to take the reins.

The Duke's hands were warm on Viola's waist as he helped her down from the cart.

For a short moment he held her in his arms, then, reluctantly, he let her go.

Viola felt the ground beneath the thin satin dancing shoes she had borrowed from Meg but wondered if her legs would support her.

How could she bear to leave here?

Life was so unfair.

If only she was still a poor girl with an absent father and no prospects!

Then perhaps she could have hoped that the Duke might one day return her feelings.

He offered Viola his arm and together they entered the barn.

The warmth and the noise that suddenly surrounded them was a pleasant change from the damp rainy evening outside.

Glowing lanterns swung from the rafters with the movement sending the dancers' shadows spiralling around the walls.

At the side of the barn, on a platform made of straw bales, an elderly man was standing and playing a fiddle, his foot beating time to the music.

And in a distant corner a younger man was tuning a set of bagpipes.

The music was bright and cheerful and in the centre of the barn several couples were dancing vigorously with the men's kilts swinging, the women in their best dresses, skipping and laughing while the music told them to change direction, swing their partners and parade around the room.

All was noise and excitement.

Viola found herself grasping the Duke's arm.

"Oh, how lovely!" she exclaimed.

The Duke nodded his head, his dark eyes gleaming with pleasure at her spontaneous delight.

"I so hoped that you would enjoy the sight. Now, I suggest that you leave your wrap over there on yon chair and dance with me!"

"But I don't know the steps."

The Duke laughed, his usually stern face relaxing.

For a second or two, Viola could see what he must have looked like when he was just a young boy, visiting his grandfather, running wild and free across the heather with his friends from the fishing village.

He would have had no cares and no worries.

It was a far cry from then to the Duke of Glentorran who was in danger of losing his beloved Castle and estate.

"You will soon learn them. Here – take my hand! Will you be trusting me, Viola?"

"Oh, always!" she gasped and within seconds found herself dancing in the middle of the barn.

Breathlessly she skipped along and ran, giggling as the other women made sure that she was in the right place at the right time.

Then, when she had mastered the simple steps, she gave herself up to the sheer joy of dancing with the Duke, of feeling his hand strong and warm on hers, admiring the breadth of his shoulders under the old green jacket he was wearing.

The Duke was whooping with much excitement as

the men spun their ladies into the middle of the ring, then, driven onwards by the insistent rhythm of the fiddle, leapt after them to wrap their arms round slender waists and lead them once more to the end of the dance.

He gazed down into Viola's flushed face.

She was looking breathtakingly beautiful, her blue eyes were sparkling with her golden hair flowing free from its ribbons and cascading down over her shoulders.

The Duke recognised he no longer cared that all he could offer her was a poverty-stricken estate and a Castle that was close to ruin.

He wanted to marry Lady Viola Northcombe and he was almost certain that she returned at least some of his feelings.

*

Back at Glentorran Castle, David was roaming the top floors of the vast building, exploring the dusty deserted rooms that had once housed many servants.

Now closed up and neglected, the top floors of the Castle were a rabbit warren of dark attics, hidden stairways and forgotten windows.

"David! What are you doing here? Mrs. Livesey told me where you were and I was concerned. You are still not fully recovered from your fever, you know. You could have felt faint climbing all these stairs."

Meg stood in the doorway of one of the great attics, looking at him with affection in her dark eyes.

David now pushed back his hair from his forehead, leaving a black streak of dust across his face.

"Meg! I am sorry. I had no intention of worrying anyone. I began exploring and I am only just beginning to realise that Glentorran Castle is such a vast and wonderful place."

Meg laughed.

"Aye, that is very true. And these old attics hold so much of our illustrious history. Generations of Glentorrans have stored their unwanted possessions up here."

David picked up a hideous looking vase from an old rickety table.

"To be frank, Meg, I cannot imagine anyone ever wanting to possess something as ugly as this!"

The Scottish girl laughed again.

"This attic was where my grandfather stored all the items that members of the family brought back from their travels abroad. I think that vase came from Egypt."

David examined it carefully.

"Why, it might be some ancient object and worth a fortune that would help your brother save the estate."

She sighed and reached out her hand to run a slim finger through the grime covering the porcelain.

"No, I'm afraid things like that only happen in story books, David. Look, over here in this cupboard are several tatty oil paintings from Italy. In a novel you would look at them and then tell me that they are worth thousands and thousands of guineas. But this is not a novel – this is *real* life and we are going to lose Glentorran!"

David then put down the vase and without thinking, reached to take her in his arms.

He could not bear to see this wonderful girl with all those tears on her cheeks and such sadness and despair in her eyes.

"Meg, my darling Meg. Please don't cry! Oh, Meg, I know you have not known me for very long, but I must tell you that I love you. I don't expect you to love me back, but at least let me take care of you."

He bent his head to her and gently kissed her lips.

To his total amazement she did not pull away, but wrapped her arms around his neck and returned his kisses.

"Oh, David. I love you, too. I think I have loved you from the very moment you rescued me from my hiding place behind that plant at the Brent's ball!"

"Will you marry me, sweet Meg?"

"Oh, yes, David. *Yes*!"

Tenderly he bent his head to kiss her again, then he realised she was pulling away from him.

"This is nonsense! How can we marry? You are in no position to take on a wife and I have no dowry to bring you."

David pulled her back into his arms and tightened his hold on her slim form.

"Listen to me, Meg," he replied. "Do not despair. Everything will be all right, I do promise you. Believe me, come tomorrow night, I will be able to tell you something that will lighten your heart completely and mean that we will always be together!"

*

At the ceilidh the tune from the fiddle ceased with a loud flourish of notes, the dancers laughed and clapped and made their way to the side of the barn where refreshments had been laid out on long trestle tables.

The Duke handed Viola a large glass of homemade lemonade, smiling at her flushed cheeks and tousled hair.

"You see, the dances are not that difficult, although I think perhaps they are a little rowdy for the select London ballrooms!"

Viola looked up at him, mischief in her eyes.

"I recall us dancing at just such a ball! You were certainly far less energetic than you are tonight!"

"But that was because I was hypnotised by a pair of brilliant bright blue eyes and could hardly remember how to waltz. Indeed I can hardly bear to take my eyes from you ever again!"

Viola caught her breath as she found herself staring up into dark eyes that burnt with a passion she had always longed to see.

Ever since she was old enough to consider falling in love, she had wanted a man to look at her in the way that Robert, the Duke of Glentorran was doing now.

There was no need for words.

Everything he felt for her was there in his eyes and she knew that he could read her feelings in her face just as easily.

The Duke tore his gaze from the beautiful sight in front of him and glanced round the hot crowded barn.

He realised that they were at the centre of attention and at the moment he craved for a quiet lonely spot where he could tell Viola exactly how he felt about her.

He took the glass of lemonade from her and placed it on a nearby table.

"Please walk with me down to the harbourside," he murmured. "I want to speak to you and what I have to say is for you and you *alone* to hear."

Drawing her arm through his he turned to the door.

Just at that moment, one of the fishermen came up and touched his forehead in salute.

He muttered a request to the Duke, who frowned in exasperation, then turned to Viola and muttered,

"Dear girl, will you excuse me for a minute or two. Apparently a stupid dispute has broken out between two families over the naming of a new boat!

"They are quite capable of coming to a decision by

fisticuffs. My wise advice might make for a more peaceful atmosphere here tomorrow morning and a reduction in cut lips and black eyes!"

Viola tried not to feel bitterly disappointed.

She realised that he was the type of man for whom duty would always come before his own desires and it was one of the reasons she loved him so much.

"Of course. I quite understand. Perhaps it will be best if you choose the name instead."

The Duke squeezed her hand.

"Then I will just insist they name the boat *The Lady Viola*," he answered her with a broad smile that brought the colour to her cheeks again.

"Wait here for me, dear Viola. I shall not be long. I promise."

She watched him stride out of the barn.

He looked so wonderful.

Tall and athletic, the kilt swinging as he walked.

She turned back to the table and discovered Heather Lyall standing there serving huge slices of shortbread and hot pies to the hungry dancers.

Viola's gaze flashed over to the plaid Heather wore across her pale grey dancing dress.

And *yes!*

There, gleaming amongst the greens and blues, was the big diamond brooch that belonged to Mrs. Van Ashton.

How long ago it seemed now that she had seen that same brooch being worn by her loud-voiced, good-hearted American hostess on board that ill-fated ship, the *Stars and Stripes*.

Viola bit her lip and decided that she had no choice but to speak.

She reckoned she might be doing the wrong thing, but if the Lyall family were involved in wrecking ships that strayed too close to the coast, then she had no option but to act.

She could not have lived with herself if a life was lost because of her inaction.

"I hope you are you enjoyin' yourself, my Lady?" Heather asked her cheerfully. "It is bonny to see you here at our ceilidh. And it is so fine to watch our Lord Robert enjoying himself so much. He has seemed so worried and sad recently.

"May I take the liberty of asking you, how is your brother? Has he recovered from his illness?"

"David is nearly back to full health, thank you."

"Och, that is good news. Fergus feared he was lost to you. He looked very pale and ill when he was rescued from that wreck. But now I can tell him that all is well."

"Is your husband not with us tonight?" Viola asked, glancing around, trying to spot the fisherman's bright red hair in the throng of villagers.

Heather shook her head.

"No, my Lady. It is a grand night for the fishing. Overcast and no moon. He went out a couple of hours ago. My mother is looking after our bairn and so I can come and enjoy myself for a few hours."

She turned to serve a slice of shortbread to another hungry dancer.

Viola stood there, undecided as to what she should do next and was about to leave when Heather turned to her once more.

"Can I tempt you to a slice of shortbread, my Lady? I made it myself."

Viola shook her head.

"No, thank you. But it looks very good, Heather – I may call you Heather, I trust – I was wondering – "

She took a deep breath,

"I could not but help notice that lovely brooch you are wearing."

Heather blushed deeply and ran her fingers over the glittering stones.

"Och, I do know to a lady such as yourself, it seems perhaps a cheap nonsense, but it was a wee gift from my Fergus and so it is very dear to me."

She lowered her voice so no one else could hear.

"The fishing has been very poorly lately, my Lady, and there has been no money for fripperies. He must have been saving up the odd pennies here and there to buy this fairing from the travelling peddler who calls every year."

Viola bit her lip again.

That brooch was certainly no fairing, so Fergus had lied to Heather.

He had stolen it from the wreck, from the luggage swept up onto the beach during the storm.

But should she make this fact common knowledge?

What would happen to Fergus?

Would he be charged with stealing and imprisoned?

Oh, that would be terrible. What would happen to his wife and child if that happened?

But on the other hand this fabulous diamond brooch could not stay here in the Glentorran fishing village.

It was worth a great deal of money and it must be returned to Mrs. Van Ashton, its rightful owner.

'But even if Fergus did find the brooch, all he is guilty of is not handing it over to the authorities. It doesn't prove that he and the other fishermen are wreckers! Surely that is just Captain Howard's guilty conscience speaking.'

She turned away, heading for the door to the barn, her mind in turmoil.

In the course of a few seconds she had gone from the heights of happiness to the depths of despair.

She loved the Duke, but not only was she living a lie under his roof by not telling him about her vast fortune, she could be the very one to shatter his faith and trust in his boyhood friend.

Outside the barn the rain had cleared away leaving a fresh night with cool breezes sweeping down from the mountains.

Viola shivered.

Her warm wrap was still inside but she had no great desire to go back for it.

She gazed up at the stars that seemed to shine far more brightly in these Northern climes than they did down in London.

She was beginning to love Scotland so very much and knew it would break her heart to leave Glentorran.

But leave it she must.

Viola could hear raised voices some way away and guessed that it was where the Duke was making a decision about a name for the new fishing boat.

Suddenly, she realised that she could not wait for him and could not let him talk to her about those feelings she had seen so clearly on his face.

For once those words had been spoken, once he had declared his liking for her, she knew everything would then become more and more complicated.

No, tonight was not the time for confessions of that sort – from either of them.

Tomorrow morning, first thing, she would ask for a private interview and tell him the whole story of what had happened to her and David since the Duke had first met them in London.

Then it would be up to him what happened next, although, with a sinking heart, Viola was fairly sure of his reaction.

The Duke was indeed a proud man and he would surely see her reluctance to tell him the facts as some kind of betrayal.

But that could not be helped, Viola determined.

She did owe him the full truth before he made any declaration to her, because he was an honourable man and would feel he had to keep any promise he made.

And how could he possibly do so if the woman he had chosen turned out to be false?

She walked swiftly away from the barn to where the grey pony was tethered.

The small boy appeared as by magic.

"Will you be wantin' me to fetch the Duke for you, my Lady?" he piped up as she scrambled into the cart and reached for the reins.

"No! There will be no need to disturb him. When he is free, will you please tell him that Lady Viola felt very tired and returned to the Castle. I am sure he will not mind walking back up the hill."

"Shall I drive you, my Lady?"

The urchin looked concerned as Viola flapped the reins and urged Bolster forwards.

"Yon beast has a mind of its own!"

As unhappy as she was, Viola had to smile.

The child was tiny, but still had that genuine desire to help that she had noticed in all the Highland people she had met.

"No, thank you," she said gently, "I will be quite all right. I think the pony will know that he is heading for his stable! He'll be quite amenable as long as I keep his head pointed towards the Castle."

She soon left the fishing village behind her and, as she had supposed, Bolster now quickened his step as they climbed the path up to the Castle gates.

As the pony cart reached the front door, Viola was surprised to see so many lights on in different rooms.

It was late and she had imagined that her brother and Meg would have retired for the night.

A cold chill ran through her – could it be that David had had a relapse of his illness? Had the fever come back?

As she jumped down from the cart, Stuart appeared from the shadows to hold the pony's head.

"A visitor indoors for you, my Lady," he said, his accent sounding extremely broad and Viola had the oddest impression that he did not care for the newcomer, whoever it was.

"For me?"

"Aye. Arrived a couple of hours back. I do believe Mrs. Livesey was asked to provide a cooked meal for him. The kitchen was none too happy, I can tell you, him eatin' all the chicken that was for the Duke's lunch tomorrow."

Viola closed her ears to the servant's gossip, as she had learned to do since she was a child.

Puzzled, she hoisted her skirts and ran up the wide stone steps into the Castle.

All she could imagine was that the visitor was from London. Perhaps sent by her cousin, Edith Matthews, to make certain that she and David were as safe and well as she had said in her letter.

*

Half an hour later, the Duke ran up the same steps, his tread light and eager.

He could not wait to see Viola once more.

In his hands he held the wrap she had left behind in the barn.

He was smiling as he would have liked to have seen her driving the fat grey pony back to the Castle and proud that she was independent enough to do so on her own.

Mrs. Livesey was in the hall but he brushed past her just as she was about to speak and strode into the drawing room.

Then he stopped in surprise.

All he could now see was a stranger standing by the fireplace, holding Viola's hands in his.

A tall thickset gentleman wearing a loud checked suit that immediately marked him out as a foreigner.

"Good evening, my Lord!"

The accent was broad American.

"I'm sorry to have arrived so late, but I was anxious to catch up with Lady Viola. I only heard where she was recently."

"Sir? You have the advantage of me."

Viola pulled her hands away from the man's grasp and turned a pale expressionless face towards the Duke.

"Your Grace, may I introduce Mr. Lewis Wilder. Mr. Wilder is an American businessman who helped David and me when we were in America."

Lewis Wilder laughed loudly.

"Businessman? That's sure a quaint way of putting it, honey."

The Duke frowned at him and the wrap he was still holding in his hands was twisted violently.

How dare this man call Viola '*honey*'.

"I'm an equal partner with Lady Viola and the Earl of Northcombe," Lewis went on, apparently unconcerned that his outstretched hand was being ignored by the Duke.

"I was unaware that you had ongoing business in the States, Viola," stated the Duke, obviously puzzled. "Is it something connected to your late father?"

"Exactly! Why, that late Earl was sure a lucky guy, all right. Lady Viola and her brother are two of the richest young people in England at this very minute!"

He shot a swift glance at the Duke's white face and added with a sneer,

"A fact, I am sure that you are well aware of, your Lordship!"

CHAPTER EIGHT

Dark clouds hung over Glentorran Castle the next morning.

In the murky distance over the mountains, thunder rumbled and an occasional flash of lightning split the sky.

The air was heavy with anticipation of the rain that must surely come before the day was out.

Viola sat at her casement window, gazing out over the neglected Castle grounds.

But she did not see the weeds, overgrown bushes and clumps of thistles and brambles.

No – all she could see was the look of betrayal that had crossed the Duke's face before his training and years of authority had taken over and a shield of blank politeness covered his features.

He had spoken politely to Lewis Wilder, enquiring after his journey, making sure that he was comfortable at the inn in the village.

Then he had bade them both goodnight, and for the first time since they had met, his gaze would not meet hers.

In vain she had tried to look into his wonderful dark eyes, to convey to him that she was sorry, desperately sorry for not telling him the truth.

But it was impossible.

The Duke looked over her shoulder at some distant point, bowed politely to them both and left the room.

Only Viola would have recognised the heaviness of his tread and the slightest bend of his head, just as if all the troubles of the world were now sitting on his shoulders.

"That guy sure doesn't seem too happy with his lot in life," Lewis Wilder had commented.

"He has a lot on his mind," Viola had replied.

"Well, I expect you'll be mighty glad to be out of here and back home in London, Lady Viola. You'll never know how grateful I was to hear that you and your brother were safe."

He gave her a warm smile, too warm by a long way for Viola's liking.

She recalled at once the way he had flirted with her in America – the last thing she needed was a complication like that here in Scotland!

Lewis Wilder had taken two steps towards her, then seeing her blank expression changed his mind.

"Now I know you're both okay, we can get down to our business again. There are many decisions to be taken regarding the oil fields in Texas."

Viola had pretended to listen but all she could think about was the Duke and the way he had not looked at her.

"So, I will be heading for London tomorrow night," Lewis Wilder had then said. "I've just hired a motorcar to drive me to Glasgow so I can board the train the following morning. You and David are welcome to come with me."

Viola had murmured that she would have to see if David was well enough to undertake such a long journey, although she knew in her heart of hearts that he was indeed fit to travel.

Just as Lewis Wilder was leaving, he had turned to Viola and said,

"By the way, Lady Viola, there was one weird tale Captain Howard had to tell. All about wreckers bringing the ship ashore onto treacherous rocks."

"It was just a silly piece of gossip," she replied. "I believe that the Captain's crew were at fault for losing the boat and so they made up the story to cheat the insurance company."

The American had shrugged on his overcoat.

"No smoke without fire, they say. When you need money as desperately as that Dook needs it, then I reckon getting a cut-back from a gang of thieves would be very useful!"

Viola had stared at him in horror.

"Sir, that is an appalling thing to say. The Duke of Glentorran is the most honourable man I have ever met!"

Lewis Wilder sneered.

"If you say so, Viola. If you say so. Setting his cap at a young girl with as much money as you have might be considered a clever piece of work by many people!

"In my opinion you'll soon discover that the only way to avoid a lot of talk is for you to marry someone as rich as you are yourself! Well, I'll say goodnight to you. Let me know in the morning about travelling South."

After he had finally left, Viola had gone to bed, but she had not slept.

She had taken off Meg's dress and then pulled on her riding habit.

She wanted for nothing more than to get out of the Castle and walk away her troubles.

But that was impossible in the middle of the night, of course, and so she sat on the casement seat, waiting for dawn, rehearsing over and over what she would say to the Duke when they next met.

*

As the black and stormy day finally dawned, Viola made her way down the staircase and into the Great Hall.

Jenny, the little housemaid, was busy washing the stone floor and she bobbed a curtsy as Viola passed.

"Looked like a wee ghostie!" she later told the cook in the kitchen. "Pale as a sheet and no a word to me. But she wasna bein' rude, you ken. She just didna see me, she was that distracted."

Viola guessed exactly where the Duke might be and she was right.

A sliver of light was shining under the door of the small room he used as an office, situated at the back of the ground floor of the Castle.

She knew that this was where he undertook all his estate business, so that crofters and fishermen could walk in from outside without having to worry about trailing dirt and fish-scales up the stairs into the big library.

Viola stood stock still for a few moments outside the door, her hand raised, but unable to knock.

She realised that this was the end of all her dreams.

The next several minutes would seal her fate and within the week she would have left this wonderful Castle, left the man she loved and be back in the mad hurly-burly of London, living an arid desolate life.

'But I have brought all this on my own head,' she thought sadly. 'The Duke is not to blame. I should have trusted him and told him the whole truth about the money from the very beginning.'

Taking a long deep breath and summoning all her courage, she knocked hard on the door and heard the quiet "come in" from the man she loved so much.

The Duke was sitting at his desk, his head on one hand.

The curtains were still drawn against the new day as the oil lamp threw a gold light against his dark tousled hair.

He looked up sharply as Viola entered the room and she almost gasped at the pain she saw etched on his face.

She so hoped that he could see how much she was suffering as well.

"*Robert* – !"

Impulsively she reached out her hand towards him and then let it drop wearily to her side.

"I would like to explain – "

"My dear Lady Viola, there is no need for any kind of explanation," the Duke interrupted her. "I am delighted to hear of your good fortune and only so sorry that you and your brother found it necessary to play us for country fools for so long."

Viola groaned at his words.

"Robert, my Lord, I never – we never – and please don't blame David for this situation! He had wanted to tell Meg immediately, but I asked him to wait."

"So you could laugh at our expense – ?"

He stood up, his face taut with anger, and he strode round to Viola's side of the desk.

He reached out, his hands grasping her shoulders.

"What did you intend, Lady Viola? To go back to London and tell all your friends about your latest conquest? To giggle at us and gossip about how poor we are here in Glentorran and how anyone would be foolish to lend us the money to repair the Castle!"

"*No*!"

Viola moaned, as his fingers were hurting the soft flesh of her upper arms.

"How can you think such a thing of me, Robert? I

106

was stupid, I know that now. But it was so hard to find a time to tell you about the money."

"*What* – all the moments we were alone together? Would it have been so very difficult to mention that you and your brother are millionaires?"

Viola could now no longer hold back the tears that began to run down her cheeks.

"I wanted to, oh, Robert, I wanted to. But I thought you would – would – "

How could she possibly finish 'you would not love me because people would just think you were only after my money'?

"It's only money, Robert," she mumbled miserably. "I am still the same person I was when you first met me at Charlotte's ball."

"So *when* were you going to tell me?" the Duke demanded. "By God, Viola. I was going to propose to you last night! Would you have told me when the engagement was announced in *The Times* and I had become the object of universal censure and a figure of fun?"

And in his fury he bent his head and kissed her on her lips, hard and angrily.

Viola felt the world slipping away, then she realised that there was little love in his kiss – just despair.

Sobbing, she pulled away, broke his grasp and fled from the room.

'Oh, how can he be so cruel!' she moaned, choking back the tears as she ran up the stairway to her room, her hand clasped across the lips he had bruised so easily.

All she wanted now was to get away from here as fast as she could.

But, first of all, she needed to speak to her brother,

because he was as much involved in this problem as she was herself.

She tapped urgently on David's door, but there was no reply.

Turning the handle she went in, but the room was empty and she could see that the sketchbook that was never more than inches from his hand was missing.

She ran next door into her own room and sank onto the bed in despair. She could hardly think clearly for the whirl of emotions in her head.

She and David must leave the Castle *immediately*!

She would go to the village, find Lewis Wilder and tell him that they would be joining him on the long journey South.

She glanced round the room.

There was nothing of her own to pack, of course, as everything here belonged to Meg.

She would have to send back what she was wearing once she arrived in London and could buy new clothes.

Viola walked to the window and gazed out towards the distant mountains. The clouds were still lying in heavy folds over the jagged peaks and she could hear thunder in the distance.

The wind was beginning to howl around the turrets of Glentorran Castle.

A violent summer storm was on its way.

This was the sort of day to stay indoors, reading by a roaring fire, eating buttered scones and crumpets.

But even when Glentorran was wet and windy, she still loved every inch of it so much and it broke her heart to think she would never see it again.

How she just longed to be here in the middle of the winter with thick snow lying on the slopes, log fires would burn in the vast grates and a huge Christmas tree would be standing proudly in the Great Hall.

Even more than that, she longed to be here for the New Year's celebrations.

Hogmanay!

The Duke had told her so many fascinating tales of what happened at that wonderful celebration on New Year's Eve.

Viola knew that wherever she was in the world in the future, once the clock had struck midnight and the New Year began, she would think of Glentorran Castle and the man she had loved and lost.

She brushed away more tears.

Well, there was one thing that she could do before she left.

After she had spoken to Lewis, she would seek out Fergus Lyall and confront him about the diamond brooch his wife was wearing, the brooch that had belonged to Mrs. Van Ashton.

For a brief moment she lingered on Lewis Wilder's words.

The Duke had told her that he would do anything to safeguard his estate.

She could never believe that he could be personally involved in any crime, but would he turn a blind eye to his people making money in that way?

Viola could remember so well all the silly schemes her late father had undertaken.

Some of them had sailed very close to the wind.

He, too, had been desperate for money and she had often wondered if occasionally he had stepped over the line between what was legal and what was not.

*

David, the Earl of Northcombe, was sitting on his favourite seat looking out to sea.

The collar of the jacket he had borrowed from the Duke, when he had been rescued from the sinking ship was turned up against the wind that was bringing the heavy rain clouds across the moors from the distant mountains behind him.

The wind had ruffled his hair into an unruly mass of tiny curls, but he was totally indifferent this morning to his appearance.

His sketchbook, very nearly full now, was open at a blank page as he was trying desperately to capture the wild scene of waves crashing over the jagged rocks with black clouds hovering against the horizon.

A soft touch on his shoulder made him turn.

Meg was standing there, a plaid draped across her head.

"David?"

"Meg! What are you doing out in this foul weather? You'll catch your death of cold."

Meg laughed.

"Och, David, this is nothing to what we experience in the winter. Just a summer storm. It will be bad later this afternoon and then it will all blow over and tomorrow will be a fine day."

She sat on the bench next to him and leant across to inspect the sketchbook.

"What a lot of drawings you have done since you arrived here. Och, I like this one of the Castle – and this – where is this? Oh, yes, it is the inside of our attics! It looks like an illustration from a book of ghost stories!"

"I like the way all your old belongings have been piled up together over the centuries with plenty of cobwebs hanging everywhere. A good artist could have done more with the depth and contrast, but I like to sketch quickly – to catch the flavour of what I see at that second."

Meg continued to flick through the pages, smiling quietly as she found several pictures of herself and of her brother and Viola.

"Oh, and here is more still life. I do so like them, David. Here are those old oil paintings and the vase from Egypt my ancestors brought to Scotland. The sketches are very good, David. You have such talent."

He hardly glanced at the page as he cast a nervous sideways glance at his dearest Meg.

"I must admit I am rather surprised to discover you are talking to me this morning, Meg. I am sure you have heard the news that broke last night when Lewis Wilder arrived at the Castle.

"The secret that Viola and I have kept is now out, but at least you know that I had already promised faithfully to tell you the truth today."

Meg nodded serenely.

"I don't really understand why Robert is so upset. So you and Viola are wealthy. That does not change you into different people. You are still David, who is a good artist and doesn't like our Scottish haggis! How is a great deal of money going to change either of those things?"

"We never wanted the money," David said, taking one of her hands between his own. "I would willingly give it all away tomorrow if I thought that was the right thing to do."

"But David – think of all the good you can do with it!"

"I know. Viola and I talked of nothing else on the voyage home from America."

Meg edged herself a little closer to him and sighed in satisfaction as his arm closed round her shoulders.

"Meg – the money means one thing and one thing only to me. I can travel abroad now. Take my paints and just sail away."

He felt the slim body next to his quiver in distress.

"I will miss you, David."

"But, Meg, I cannot go unless you come with me! Marry me, Meg. *Please* marry me. You just cannot let me travel out to the South Seas on my own!"

He bent his head and kissed her.

Meg's arms crept round his neck and for an ecstatic moment she gave herself up to his embrace.

Then, reluctantly, she pulled away, tears filling her eyes.

"Oh, David. I love you so much. I would be very honoured to be your wife. I would be quite happy if we were as poor as church mice, if we had to live on coconuts and fish and live in a little grass hut on a tropical island! I would willingly travel to the other side of the world with you, but *I can't.*"

David went pale.

His arms tightened round her, refusing to let her go.

"Why, Meg? What can stop us? Surely you are not worried about what people will say?"

She shook her head, the plaid slipping down around her shoulders.

"No, I care nothing for public opinion, but David, how can I possibly leave Robert to carry the whole burden of Glentorran all by himself?"

"But I have so much money now. You could give Robert enough to make a difference and – "

"Hush, my dear!"

She placed slim fingers over his lips.

"Robert would never dream of taking a penny from me, knowing that it had come from you. No, not even to save Glentorran!"

Meg stood up, pulling the plaid over her dark hair to protect herself from the wind that was now bringing fine drizzle to the cliffs of Glentorran.

David leapt to his feet, trying to hold her back.

"Don't go, Meg!"

But she just shook her head, fighting back the tears that glistened in her dark eyes.

"There is just no point in talking about it any more, David. I am Lady Margaret Glentorran and I know that if I betray my birthright and don't stay to help my brother save the Castle, then I would never be truly happy again, even with you, the man I love!"

And without another word, she turned and ran back up the winding path towards the Castle.

*

Viola pulled on her riding jacket and walked slowly down the stone steps and out of the Castle.

She now needed to speak urgently to Lewis Wilder, because she had made a decision and needed to put it into action without a moment's delay.

The American had taken a room at the local village inn, *The Glentorran Arms*.

When he had arrived at the Castle, he had explained to Viola that it was imperative that she and David return to London to attend to all the documents and decisions that needed their approval.

Viola groaned.

Yes, she tended to forget that she was no longer a carefree maiden with nothing to worry about except if she could afford to buy a new ball gown and the hole in her dancing shoes.

Now she was the owner of a vast business empire with hundreds of employees whose livelihood depended on the decisions she and her brother made.

She could no longer escape these responsibilities.

This magical time in Scotland had come to an end.

She crossed the neglected garden, the wind blowing branches across her path, long tendrils of unpruned roses reaching out to catch her sleeves and skirt.

As she reached the wooden gate that led to the cliff path, she was startled as Meg rushed through it and hurried past her without a word, holding her plaid across her face.

A few seconds later, David appeared, looking pale and upset, clutching his sketchbook.

"Viola! Have you seen Meg?"

"Yes, she just passed me. She seemed very upset. Have you two argued? Surely not."

David laughed, but it was not a happy sound, it was bitter and angry.

"No, it wasn't an argument. I want to marry Meg, but even though she has no problems with my fortune, she knows that Robert will never accept a penny from her if it comes from me. And she refuses to leave the Duke while he is having all these problems with the Castle.

"I thought that inheriting a fortune would bring us nothing but happiness. *How wrong I was!*"

Viola shuddered.

"I fear the Glentorrans will be glad to see the back of us," she said sadly.

"Well, they will not have long to wait. I am heading to the village now to speak to Lewis Wilder and ask him to arrange for us to travel down to London with him when he leaves tonight. All the business he wishes to discuss with us can be done once we are safely back home with Cousin Edith."

"Tonight!"

"Yes, David, the sooner we are away from here the better. Every time Robert looks at me with so much dislike and contempt, I – "

She stopped, a sob breaking from her throat.

Her twin looked at her gravely and then said,

"Viola, I am not coming to London with you."

"*Not* coming?"

David suddenly looked taller and older, very much an Earl of the Realm, all his youthful hesitancy gone.

"Viola, whatever is between you and the Duke is your business. I shall not pry. But I love Meg and I know that once I leave here, I will never have the chance to prove to her how much I care."

"But the money will *always* come between you!"

David nodded his head, as he abstractedly flicked through the sketchbook, staring down at the little drawings he had made of the girl he loved.

"If I have to give it all away, then so be it! I will do everything in my power to win the woman I love."

"But you cannot stay here at the Castle? Where on earth will you live?"

He smiled.

"I am quite sure that I can find rooms in the village. I shall sketch and paint and sell my work to visitors. I shall not use a penny of my fortune and eventually my darling Meg will realise that I am never going to leave."

Viola sighed.

She could not blame David for his decision.

She knew that he passionately hated the thought of being a businessman. It would surely kill him to take on the responsibilities that she now faced.

But oh, if only she could do the same, but she knew that was impossible.

How could she contemplate living just a mile away from Robert, perhaps seeing him regularly in the village, watching him as he struggled with the estate and the Castle and being unable to help?

It would be more than she could bear.

She reached up and kissed David's cheek.

"Meg is a very lucky girl," she whispered. "And I am certain it will not be long before she realises it."

She turned away.

"Please tell Mrs. Livesey, David, that I will not be in for luncheon."

He glanced up in concern at the dark clouds racing across the sullen sky.

"You are going to get wet, Viola! Wait just a few minutes until this squall has passed. I don't like the look of the weather coming in from those mountains. Meg says these summer storms can be very intense."

Viola shook her head vigorously.

All she wanted was to be as far away as possible from the Castle, before the Duke appeared again and she had to see the cold condemnation on his face.

"It's only water. I won't melt. Goodness, remember how wet we got when the ship sank? I'll run all the way! If there's any lightning, I promise I will take shelter, don't worry. There is no way I can come to harm between here and the village."

David watched as she vanished down the driveway leading to the cliff path and then he climbed the steep stone steps up to the front door of the Castle.

CHAPTER NINE

Robert, the Duke of Glentorran, was an angry man – angry with Viola, but really furious with himself.

He had kissed the girl against her will!

That was the mark of a cad, a rotter, a man whom decent Society should shun.

Whistling up his dogs he stormed out of the Castle, headed across the gardens and out onto the moors.

Oblivious of the rain that was now falling heavily, he strode on through the heather, slashing with his stick at the odd thistle and bramble that dared to snag his kilt as he passed.

Yes, he had kissed her, but she deserved it!

He loved her so much and she had played with his affections, made a fool of him and hurt him so badly that he did not think he could ever recover.

He suddenly recalled the old gypsy who had visited the Castle one Christmas, telling fortunes to him, Meg and their guests.

She had told him he would have his heart broken by a man from across the water.

He had laughed at the time, paying the old woman her fee, but privately thinking to himself what rubbish this fortune-telling seemed.

But now –

The Duke pushed his wet hair out of his eyes and stared through the veils of rain towards the tumultuous sea.

Well, she had been right!

When that American, Lewis Wilder, had told him last night about the fortune that Viola and her brother now owned, he had felt his heart break into a thousand pieces.

He had been about to propose marriage to her, but how could he now ask for her hand in marriage?

The world would believe that he was an adventurer, a man who was prepared to live off his wife's money.

And Society would never believe that he had fallen in love with a beautiful young girl who he had thought was penniless – like him.

No, they would all snigger and point behind their hands and he would find it difficult to hold his head up in company again.

He was far too proud to even contemplate such a situation for one single moment.

If *only* he did not love Viola so much!

Everything about her was perfection to him.

Her smile, her sense of humour, the way she was so interested in everything she saw round her, the long golden hair and such brilliant blue eyes, her ability to understand and sympathise with people from all walks of life.

Yes, she was his perfect woman and just when he thought she was within his reach, he realised that it had all been just a game to her.

Surely she could just have told him of her change in circumstances as soon as they had met.

Would that not have been the natural and kind thing to do?

Sighing, he whistled to the dogs that were happily sniffing for rabbits in the wet heather and turned back to the Castle.

He stared down at that wonderful building – even

half hidden by mist, he could see all the magnificent turrets and spires.

This was his heritage and he wondered bitterly how long he could keep the wolf from the door.

The Duke's expression was grim.

'I should have gone ahead and asked Viola to marry me,' he mused. 'That is just what most men in my position would have done and be damned to any gossip. I used to say I would do anything to save Glentorran – but that is a step too far.'

A sudden crack of thunder made him recognise that the big storm that had been brewing all morning had finally reached Glentorran.

The skies had darkened to a purple hue and the sea was grey and angry-looking, covered with white crests as the wind tossed the waves around.

With a face as black as the storm, the Duke turned and strode back down the slope towards the Castle.

He was very sure that Viola and her brother would soon leave Glentorran.

He knew that his sister would be upset, but for now he could not worry about that.

"The sooner they leave here the better," he snapped at his astonished dogs.

"*Wretched girl!*"

He stamped into the Great Hall, dripping water all over the black and white tiles.

Mrs. Livesey hurried to meet him.

"Och, Your Grace. It's soaked through you are!"

The Duke shrugged away her concern.

"Just a little water, Mrs. Livesey. Don't fuss! Can you inform Lady Viola that I would like to speak to her in the study immediately, please."

Mrs. Livesey frowned.

"Lady Viola is away to the village, Your Grace."

He stared at her.

"What? When did she go?"

"I – I am not sure, Your Grace."

"Did she ride or take the pony cart?"

Mrs. Livesey shook her head.

"No, I believe she walked, Your Grace."

The Duke now swung round and headed back to the great studded entrance door.

He flung it open and stared out at the driving rain.

Flashes of lightning forked through the sky whilst thunder rolled and crashed overhead.

A feeling of dread ran through his body.

Suddenly it did not seem to matter that Viola had not told him the truth about her fortune.

All that mattered was that the woman he loved so passionately was out there alone in that tempest.

Without another word, he ordered his dogs to stay, then plunged out of the door and headed at full speed down the drive, across the grounds towards the cliff path leading to Glentorran village.

*

The storm coming in from the mountains was still several miles away over the mountains when Viola reached the outskirts of Glentorran village.

She glanced up at the threatening sky, but she was so miserable that the dark clouds made no difference to her.

She resolutely refused to turn around and gaze back up the hill to where the Castle stood, its spires and turrets reaching for the sky.

No, that was a place she no longer had any right to look at or love.

That was Robert's home, his *Castle of Dreams* and nothing to do with her.

All she wanted was to reach *The Glentorran Inn*, find Lewis Wilder and arrange her journey to London.

And she would be on her own, because David was determined to stay here in Scotland and fight for Meg, the girl he loved.

Viola felt more tears burning her eyes and brushed them away.

This was all her fault.

She should have told Robert the truth straight away instead of wanting the luxury of his friendship for just one more day.

As she rounded the final corner, she stopped.

Heather Lyall, Fergus's wife, was standing by the side of the road, a large wicker basket at her feet.

"Heather! Good morning."

The Scottish girl dropped a small bob curtsy.

"Lady Viola! Whatever are you doing out in this weather? Och, you'll be soaked through. This drizzle will become a fearful storm very soon."

Viola laughed shakily.

"I certainly won't melt away! And I intend to be indoors very soon. But what about you?"

Heather pulled her plaid over her head to keep the rain from her hair.

"I'm here waitin' for the local omnibus. One runs every week through Glentorran. It's market day today in Corraig, our local town. I'm in need of several things our shops in the village cannot supply."

Viola nodded.

"And is Fergus looking after Ian?"

Heather laughed out loud.

"Och no. Fergus has gone to anchor his boat further out into the harbour in deeper water where it will be safer when the storm arrives. My mother is looking after wee Ian."

She sighed, the happiness draining from her pretty face, as she continued,

"Our boat is gettin' old – it belonged to Fergus's father and has been repaired so many times that it's hardly sea-worthy now. I'm always terrified it will founder one day when he is out at sea.

"That is why he hasn't gone out fishin' today. The boat needs a new rudder badly and Fergus cannot fish until it is fitted."

"And there is no money for a new boat?"

Heather shook her head.

"No indeed. We make just enough from the fish to live on, but a new boat costs a fortune and that we do not have!"

Viola hesitated.

She could see so clearly the great diamond brooch pinned into Heather's plaid.

Surely if Fergus had stolen it from the Van Ashtons then he would realise its value and not give it to his wife to wear?

Suddenly Viola made up her mind.

Not speaking out when she should have done had caused her so much grief recently. She was not going to let this opportunity slip past.

"Heather – I do hope you will not be offended by my question, but – "

The Scottish girl looked puzzled.

"Och, ask what you like, Lady Viola."

"That brooch you are wearing – "

Heather's pretty face broke into a wide smile.

"I can guess what you are going to say!"

"Can you?"

Viola was startled.

"Aye. I told you that Fergus had bought the brooch from a pedlar, didn't I? Well, I was wrong. He let slip the other night that he didn't even have enough money to buy me a wee present, but he still wanted me to believe he had. Silly man! As if it would bother me when things are so difficult with the fishin'!"

Viola frowned.

"So you know where the brooch came from?"

"Och, yes. It was a gift from that American lady, Mrs. Van Ashton, for helpin' to save her and her husband from the ship that dreadful night. He didn't tell me at first because he thought I would be cross that he had received a gift because, of course, you do not expect recompense for savin' lives."

Viola felt a wave of pure relief wash over her.

A *gift*!

Why had she never thought of that?

Heather looked concerned.

"You're not to worry, Lady Viola. It's only a silly trifle made of paste. And look – here comes the omnibus. I'll be glad to get in out of the rain."

And she waved down the bus which came chugging around a bend, full of women on their way to market, black smoke billowing from its exhaust.

Before Viola could speak, Heather nimbly jumped on board and, as the rain began to fall more heavily, the omnibus rattled and groaned its way along the road up the hill and out of sight.

Viola found herself smiling to herself, despite her breaking heart.

She knew that she would have to send a message to Fergus and Heather before she left Glentorran.

If they sold that brooch, there would be plenty of money for a new boat!

'Well, that at least is one good thing I can do for Glentorran,' she thought as she pulled up the collar of her jacket more tightly around her neck.

The rain was driving in now on the wind and Viola turned her steps towards *The Glentorran Arms*.

She now had to find Lewis Wilder and arrange her transport away from this magical place and away from the man who so obviously despised her.

*

Back in the Castle, David was sitting in the library, moodily glancing through his sketchbook.

Outside thunder rumbled closer and closer and the windows rattled loudly in their frames as the storm began to gather strength.

He hoped Viola had reached *The Glentorran Arms* safely. But he was sure that she would be fine as she had had plenty of time to get indoors.

David knew he should be upstairs packing, because it was obvious that he could not stay in the Castle once his twin sister had left.

'Oh, darling Meg, how am I ever going to win you as my wife?' he mused.

'If I was give to away every penny I own, would that help? Would your brother let you marry me if I could not even afford to put a roof over your head? I think *not*!'

But he was still determined not to give in.

He had already worked out his plan of campaign.

He would sell the majority of his shares in the oil company – either to Lewis Wilder or to someone else.

He was quite certain there would be no scarcity of buyers.

He would keep enough to live on, find lodgings in Glentorran and concentrate on his art.

All his dreams of travelling abroad would have to be abandoned for the present.

But one day he was quite certain that he and Meg would have their own adventures and travel together to the South Seas.

Absently he now turned over the earliest pages of the sketchbook.

When Mrs. Livesey had found him a book to draw in, she had asked him to be careful as there were already sketches in the front of the book.

David had never looked at them before.

He had vaguely believed that they had been drawn by another visitor to the Castle and so had no interest for him.

Now as he turned over the pages, he realised he was looking at sketches of paintings.

How very strange and who would bother to sketch detailed drawings of someone else's art?

"But I recognise these!" he called out aloud. 'These are the paintings up in the Castle attics, the ones covered in dirt and dust.'

He flicked swiftly forward through the book to find the charcoal sketch he had made a few days before.

Yes, there were the same pieces of artwork, but he had only indicated a rough outline of the figures. He had not even bothered to take off the dust sheets that covered most of the paintings.

He had liked the shrouded shapes and only detailed the one closest to him.

He had made a clearer sketch of the old Egyptian vase Meg had shown him, but it was not what excited him now.

These drawings were very clear and as he looked at them, he began to feel a shiver of excitement run through his body.

The colours – the shape of the figures – surely these had not been painted by an amateur.

These were wonderful paintings drawn, he was sure, by an Old Master of the Italian School.

David leapt to his feet and headed out of the door, calling for Meg.

He had to go up to the attics immediately!

*

When the storm eventually broke over the village, Viola was only yards from *The Glentorran Arms*.

The inn stood back a little way from the quayside that ran around the harbour.

Waves were beginning to swell and crash over the sea wall casting their spray over a wide arc.

Luckily the fishing fleet was not in the harbour.

They were anchored out at sea.

Viola could understand why Fergus had decided to move his boat.

There was a small dinghy tied onto the harbour wall and every time the waves rushed in from the sea, the boat smashed against the unyielding stone sea wall.

Viola sheltered her eyes from the stinging rain and gazed across the harbour.

Through the gloom she thought she could just make out the shape of Fergus's boat, anchored safely away from the land.

Another roll of thunder made her flinch.

The storm was almost on top of the village now.

But even as she turned round to hasten into the inn, she knew that no amount of bad weather would ever make her love Glentorran the less.

'But it isn't just the place itself I love so much,' she whispered. 'It is *Robert*, the life and heart of the estate.

'Oh, Robert, I love you with all my heart. You will never know how deeply I honour and respect you and how devastated I am that you think so badly of me.'

With hot tears mingling with the cold raindrops on her face, she turned once more to gaze out at the sea.

Just then a wild flash of lightning streaked through the overcast sky.

The brilliant light illuminated the dark quayside for a second and a movement caught Viola's eye.

Then the light was gone and gloom descended once more.

Viola hesitated.

She was so wet and desperate to reach cover.

But that movement had been odd – out of place.

'Just a stray dog,' she tried to tell herself, straining her eyes to see through the rain.

But it had been far too slow to be a dog running for cover and too big for a cat or even a bird desperate to find shelter.

With an ear-splitting noise that made her wince, the thunder crashed again and the lightning flashed, zigzagging across the rolling clouds.

And to Viola's great horror, she could now see that the movement was a small boy, walking cheerfully through the rain towards the steps that lead down to the water from the harbour edge.

A very small boy, about three years old.

Gasping with fear, Viola now realised that it was little Ian Lyall, the Duke's Godson.

"Ian! *Stop*! Ian! Oh, help, someone help me!"

But the village street and harbour were deserted, of course. The men all at sea and most of the women indoors or, like Heather, gone to the market.

Viola ran like the wind towards the child.

Where was his grandmother?

How had he escaped from her cottage?

But there was no time to think of such questions.

Even as she ran, she knew she would not be in time.

The little boy was clambering down the steps out of her sight.

With a sob Viola flung herself forward and skidded down the slippery seaweed-covered steps.

To her relief she saw that the child was not in the water, but had stepped into the dinghy she had seen earlier.

Babbling away happily to himself, oblivious of the pouring rain, he was playing at some silly game, obviously pretending to fish like this father.

"Ian – sweetheart – give me your hand," she called out, trying to keep her voice calm so as not as to upset the red-headed infant.

She reached forward, trying to balance on the steps, but she just could not reach into the dinghy, it was bobbing around too violently in the rough water.

Ian turned and gave her a wide grin.

He was plainly not the slightest bit concerned, but had no intention of climbing out of the little boat.

"Ian! Come out of there at once. Oh, what shall I do? Where is everyone?"

Viola made up her mind.

No one was going to come to her aid.

Being careful not to slip into the water, she stepped into the dinghy.

She would have to pick up the little boy before she could climb back out onto solid ground once more.

The child laughed and clapped his hands playfully as she took a tentative step forward and then groaned as her foot slid on a coating of fish scales and she sat down with a bump.

For a second a sharp pain shot through her left foot as she struggled onto her knees and reached for Ian.

Just then the thunder rolled again, the storm sent a vicious gust of wind and the dinghy bucked and rolled like a wild horse.

Viola reached out and pulled Ian into her arms.

She turned to climb out of the boat and then gave a little groan of despair.

The last lurch of the tossing boat had loosened the rope that moored it to a large iron ring set into the harbour wall.

Even as she looked in horror, the rope end slipped through and splashed down into the water.

Like a horse freed from its tether, the boat turned right round and within seconds was yards away from land, heading out across the harbour and towards the open sea!

CHAPTER TEN

Viola moaned as the dinghy rocked violently in the rough water.

She hunted frantically for the oars, but realised that the little boat had none.

Waves were already beginning to slop in over the sides and young Ian was suddenly beginning to sense that his adventure was not so much fun any more.

Viola could see that his bottom lip was trembling and she was terrified that the child would start to panic.

Swiftly she leant straight forward and picked him up, cradling him in her lap, trying to protect him from the worst of the wind and rain.

"Hush, Ian. Don't cry, sweetheart. Everything will be all right. Sit quietly, there's a good boy."

She stared around in horror.

The dinghy was heading slowly but surely towards the harbour entrance, carried there by the turning tide.

Viola cast frantic glances back at the shoreline, but there was no one in sight.

Except – yes, through all the spray she could see a figure running headlong down the cliff path and, even as she watched, the rain eased for a moment and she could see it was a man.

It was the Duke!

Even as she watched, the Duke flung off his jacket and without hesitating dived into the choppy grey water.

'Oh, Robert! Oh, my love! Be very careful. Oh, God *please*, please take care of him, in your infinite mercy, take care of Robert Glentorran!'

Viola prayed desperately as she had never prayed in her entire life.

She watched in growing despair as the Duke's dark head disappeared again and again beneath the water, until his strong arms lifted him up once again above the white crests of the raging waves as he battled on towards her.

She knew that she dared not even try to help.

It was all she could do to keep the boat on an even keel as it was thrown around by the waves.

And she had to protect Ian.

How could she ever face Heather and Fergus if she let anything happen to their precious son?

But oh, Robert was in such danger.

How could she go on living if anything happened to him?

Then just as the Duke seemed to be losing his battle and she feared that the sea was about to swallow him up, an answer came to her prayers.

The black clouds broke apart – just for an instant – a beam of sunlight touched the sea like a golden finger and the wind dropped to a gentle breeze.

It was enough for the waves to calm and for him to make one last desperate surge forwards towards the little dinghy.

The Duke caught hold of the mooring rope floating behind the dinghy and with that to help him, he managed to edge himself alongside, his hands tightening over the side of the boat that contained everything he held so dear.

He looked up at Viola and to her astonishment, she realised he was smiling!

"Lady Viola, may I presume? May I make so bold as to enquire, what is this passion you have for immersing yourself and your friends in sea water at regular intervals?"

"Oh, Robert, I was so frightened you were going to drown!"

The Duke grinned again, looking so very handsome with his black hair plastered against his forehead.

"In this harbour? I don't think so. Fergus and I used to race across it every time I came to Glentorran when I was a lad. We even swam across here on Christmas Day last year when we had to break the ice!

"Now listen, Viola, I want you to sit on the far side of the boat and hold Ian very still.

"And you, young man, you just go on being a brave wee laddie and we'll soon have you home."

Viola edged carefully along the wooden seat and, as the sun vanished once more behind the clouds and the wind began roaring wildly again, the Duke heaved himself into the dinghy, his shirt sticking to his body like a second skin.

For a moment Viola forgot that she and the Duke were no longer friends and she reached out a hand to brush the soaking wet hair from his eyes.

At the same time his right hand was raised to do the same and their fingers touched and entwined.

Viola felt her breath catch in her throat as she gazed into those dark eyes she loved so much.

But this was no time for talking or to say what was causing her heart to feel so heavy.

The dinghy lurched wildly sideways as another gust of wind caught it in its grip.

She looked behind her and groaned in horror to see the harbour entrance coming closer and closer.

The sea was certainly rough enough here inside the

sheltering arms of the cliffs, but what a brutal maelstrom it would be outside the harbour.

"Robert, what shall we do? How are we going to get back to the shore?"

The Duke scowled.

"Look, over there – that's Fergus' fishing boat. He always moors it in deep water when there is a storm. He'll be on board. If we can get there, we'll be safe!"

"Dada!"

Ian shouted suddenly and pointed.

True enough, they could see Fergus standing by the rails, staring in anguish to where his son was being carried away by the wind and tide.

"If only we had oars!"

The Duke swore under his breath and then reaching forward, he smashed both his fists down hard on the other wooden seat.

Viola screamed as splinters flew in the air, but the wood, which was obviously half-rotten, broke away easily and he seized the plank to use as an oar.

His powerful shoulders sent the boat flying through the water towards Fergus.

"Robert, well done. You have saved us!"

He shook his head grimly as he paddled furiously, trying to keep the dinghy on a straight course.

"Not yet, my darling girl, not yet. Look! You can see the currents swirling round the fishing boat. The water is deep there and treacherous. I fear we will only have one chance to get Ian on board."

Viola's lips set in a firm line and she held the child tightly in her arms.

She recognised that they were in grave danger, but

her heart was dancing because the Duke had called her his *'darling girl'*!

"Just tell me what to do."

"Look now, Fergus has dropped a rope ladder down over the side. As soon as we reach it, I will try and hold the dinghy still. He will climb down as far as he can. Hand Ian to him and then Fergus can help you up."

"But what about you. Robert, I am *not* leaving you. I shall never leave you!"

His gaze pierced her through to her very soul.

"Viola, my dearest, you must save yourself. Trust me. If you have any feelings for me at all, please do now exactly as I ask."

"I will trust you for all eternity," whispered Viola and then there was no more time for speaking.

The dinghy swung on the current and slid alongside the fishing boat.

There was Fergus, balancing himself at the end of the rope ladder with the skill of a man who spent his whole life at sea, holding out one arm.

Before Viola could think, she was standing up and, swaying violently, she managed to lift the child and thrust him into his father's welcoming arms.

With a sob of relief, Viola watched as Fergus ran up the ladder and placed his son down somewhere on the deck.

Then he scrambled back down the ladder, reaching out towards her.

"Quickly, Lady Viola. Take my hand!"

"Viola! You must jump. *Now!*"

The Duke's voice was anguished with concern.

But as she readied herself to leap onto the swinging ladder, a vicious blast of tumultuous wind sent the dinghy spiralling away from the fishing boat.

And with a scream she tumbled backwards into the cold water that was now fast filling the little boat.

The next few minutes always lived in Viola's mind as a terrifying nightmare.

It was as if the storm, now cheated of one victim, was determined to do its worst and the wind and rain blew the dinghy, spinning like a top, out of the harbour entrance where the giant waves took hold of it.

Viola felt the Duke's strong arms fasten around her, holding her safe against him.

She was aware that his lips grazed her forehead and just as a vast wave turned the dinghy over, she heard him whisper,

"I shall love you to the end of days."

He struggled to the surface, gasping and choking.

"Viola!"

He swam a few yards and stared around in despair.

There!

With her golden hair floating around her head like a silken halo, Viola was floating in the sea.

"*Viola*!"

With a few powerful strokes the Duke reached her side.

She was unconscious and there was a raw mark on her dear forehead and he thought that she must have hit her head as the dinghy capsized.

'Oh, my Lord God, let me save her!' he prayed and supporting her limp body, he began to swim towards the distant shore, letting the current take him to what he hoped was safety.

All he knew for certain was that whatever happened in the next few seconds, he would never ever let go of his beloved again.

Viola was dreaming.

It was winter and she was skating on a frozen loch. She could feel the icy wind in her face, her feet and hands ached from the cold.

But she realised she was happy because at her side, holding her hand, was the man she loved.

And she knew that if she skated just a little faster, she would ultimately reach a safe haven where nothing and no one could harm her –

Viola's eyelids fluttered open.

She was lying shivering on a stony beach, her head pillowed on the Duke's arm.

She coughed, groaned and tried to sit up, trembling violently as the cold cut through her soaking wet clothes.

Immediately the Duke's anxious face bent over her.

"Viola! Oh, sweetheart, are you all right? Don't move. You hit your head when you went overboard. Dear Lord, Viola, I thought I had *lost* you!"

She felt his strong arms close round her as he lifted her aching head towards him.

Their kiss was everything she had ever dreamed of, a declaration of their deep true feelings for each other.

"Robert, my own love, where are we?"

The Duke gazed round him stroking the wet tangles of golden hair back from her temples.

"On a little beach along the coast from the Castle. I know it well. I played here often when I was a boy. The current swept us here when the boat capsized.

"You are so cold! But don't fret, Fergus will have raised the alarm by now and help will be on its way. We will soon have you safe and sound back at the Castle."

Viola stared into his dark eyes.

"You saved my life – " she murmured.

"Your life is *my* life," the Duke replied, his voice shaking with emotion.

He would never tell her of the anguished feeling of loss that had swept through his soul, when he had seen the girl he loved drifting away in the waves.

Yes, he had struggled with every fibre in his body to get her to shore and safety, refusing to let the angry sea claim her as its own.

"Viola, can you ever forgive me for my own stupid pride? For spoiling our friendship because of my ridiculous notions of what is right?

"When I saw you unconscious in the water, when I thought I was going to lose you, I knew that nothing in the whole world was worth turning my back on our love.

"How could I have been such a silly stubborn fool? Viola, my darling girl, could you ever love someone who is so foolish?"

The Duke kissed her again and as she drew away, Viola exclaimed with a moan of happiness,

"*I* am the one who should ask for forgiveness!

"Why on earth didn't I tell you about the wretched inheritance when we met again after the shipwreck? It was so stupid, so childish.

"David has more sense than me. He wanted to tell you and Meg immediately, but I made him promise to wait.

"I wanted your – friendship – so much. I had come to depend on it as being necessary for my very being. But I didn't trust you to like me if you knew I was wealthy.

"And then, when I realised I had to tell you because I was living a lie, the opportunity never arose.

"So, my darling man, can you ever love a girl who is so brainless!"

The Duke laughed out loud and for the first time in many weeks, the lines of strain around his eyes and mouth vanished.

"A fool of a man and a foolish girl! Well, I think we make the perfect couple, Viola.

"I don't believe anyone else would want us, so we had better marry as soon as possible!"

He knelt at her side and Viola smiled.

Soaked to the skin, he was still looking amazingly handsome.

"Lady Viola Northcombe, I, Robert, the sixth Duke of Glentorran do hereby ask you for your hand in marriage. You are my life and my heart. Please make me the happiest of men and say 'yes'!"

Viola knelt in front of him, seemingly oblivious to the sharp stones pressing on her knees, linking her hands with his, her great blue eyes shining like stars.

"I, Viola Northcombe, now pledge myself to you, Robert, the Duke of Glentorran, for ever and ever, *amen*."

Kneeling together in the pouring rain on that wild windswept beach, they kissed and knew that nothing and no one would ever part them again.

*

Three months later on a glorious autumn day, two riders were cantering over the moor through purple heather busy with bees collecting the famous Glentorran honey.

The sky above them was a pale eggshell blue and somewhere a lark hovered, its piping song cascading down towards them.

As the two riders crested the hill, they reined their mounts to a halt and stared down into the glen below.

"There!"

The Duke pointed with his whip.

"See, my darling, that is where the new hospital is being built. They have already dug the foundations and by next year the new Duchess of Glentorran Hospital will be up and running."

Viola smiled in delight, her golden hair escaping from the small, blue close-fitting hat she wore, its feather curling round to touch her cheek.

She had been so thrilled when the Duke had agreed that she could finance the construction of a hospital for the local district.

She could still remember with great amusement, the horrified look on Lewis Wilder's face when she had told him of her plans.

"But financing a hospital, Lady Viola! It will take an enormous amount of dough for years and years to come!

"Do think about it – not only the construction work, but paying doctors and nurses and from these plans you've shown me, you want an operating theatre as well!"

"Certainly!" Viola had replied firmly.

There would then be no further need for the people of Glentorran and the surrounding district to travel miles and miles for treatment.

No one would die from lack of basic medical care, not while she had a penny left in her bank account.

Lewis Wilder had been bemused and bewildered, but, seeing she could not be moved and most impressed by the glittering emerald and diamond engagement ring on her finger, had accepted defeat.

He had returned to America and Viola was sure that secretly he was quite pleased to be left in charge of the oil business out in Texas.

The Duke's business manager had agreed to keep a watching brief on how the Northcombe Oil Fields were run and Viola was certain that she could leave it in his capable hands.

She realised that she could not be involved herself.

She would have far too much to do helping Robert run the estate.

They had such great plans.

The next year would see the building of a second school in Glentorran village so that the older children could continue their education if they wished.

Her money was now being put to good use for the benefit of the district just as she had dreamed.

As their ride ended and they turned back towards the Castle, Viola reached out her hand and the Duke took it in his own.

Even when they were riding out they found every opportunity they could to be close to each other.

Stirrup to stirrup, they rode down the hill and into the Castle grounds that were now a hive of activity.

All the old gardens were being brought back to life and new beds were being carved out of the surrounding land.

A great water feature was being constructed.

A small spring high on the moors would run down through a long series of channels and lakes to cascade over a sparkling waterfall and into a deep pool where great koi carp would swim.

Architects, designers and workers from all over the district were busy every day at Glentorran.

The whole local population was feeling the benefit of the Glentorran expansion.

Jobs were being created everywhere, especially in the Castle itself.

Mrs. Livesey was now like a cat that had licked the cream – her dour expression had vanished as she was now in charge of a large and growing staff.

All the rooms that had been closed for years were being opened, cleaned and redecorated.

Once again the great kitchens were in full use and cook could be heard singing songs from popular operettas she was so happy.

The Duke had big exciting plans to open the Castle grounds to the public on certain days of the year.

There would now be a chance for people to come to see how wonderful Glentorran was and to purchase such products as plants, flowers, honey and other items made by the crofters and estate workers.

"Dear old Angus is in his element making an Italian garden to enhance the Castle grounds," Viola enthused.

"It was such a kind thought of yours, Robert, to involve him by giving him his own project. I am certain he would have been deeply upset to have all these 'foreigners' working in his gardens."

The Duke smiled.

"The Italian Garden! It is well named. I still cannot believe how much money I received for those old Italian paintings David found in the attic! A small fortune.

"To think they were sitting up there all this time, unrecognised!"

Viola laughed.

She could recall the look of bliss on her brother's face when Robert had carried her back into the Castle after their adventure in the harbour.

He had been less excited by their engagement than by his news that he was sure he had discovered a collection of very rare and extremely valuable paintings abandoned in the Glentorran attics.

"Your grandfather so obviously thought his brother, your great-uncle, had bought a load of useless rubbish with him when he returned from Italy.

"Goodness, Robert, he might have had them burnt or destroyed!"

The Duke chuckled.

"No, he was far too canny an old gentleman to ever throw anything away be it priceless paintings or old broken chairs. It was all stored away in the attics in case it came in useful some day. And Glentorran has now to thank him for his wise ways!"

They reached the drive that led to the Castle with its towers and spires reaching up to the sky.

The Duke reined to a halt and turned to look at his beautiful fiancée, his face suddenly serious.

"Next week, Viola my darling, you will become the Duchess of Glentorran. I am worried. Is it too much of a burden to ask you to bear? Life will not be easy, even with our money, and you will find that you have little time for yourself. You will belong to the people of Glentorran as much as to me."

Viola stared up at the great Castle.

It was indeed a most intimidating sight as well as a vast responsibility for someone as young as her to carry.

She turned and gazed into Robert's dark eyes.

"I cannot wait, my love," she said simply, "and we will be doing everything together, so that any burden will be shared between us."

*

Seven days later all of Glentorran was bedecked in tartan and bunting for the wedding of their beloved Duke to Lady Viola Northcombe.

The Duke had decreed that the wedding would take place in the Castle Chapel and not in a bigger Church in a faraway town where they knew no one.

He wanted everyone in Glentorran to attend if they could.

So many of the great and good of Scotland, Earls and Countesses, Dukes and Princes, crofters, fisherfolk and everyone who loved and admired the young couple, were gathered to witness the joining of two people who were so much in love.

In the front pew, resplendent in deep ruby velvet, sat Lady Margaret, now the new Countess of Northcombe, her pretty face aglow with happiness.

Her wedding to her beloved David had taken place a month earlier.

They had both shunned the idea of a Society affair, Meg insisting that she and David were a shy quiet couple and so would have a shy quiet wedding!

But now she was bubbling with excitement because after the ceremony, they would be setting out on their big adventure, the one they had dreamed of for so long.

They were heading out across Europe and intending to travel through Africa, on to India and then to the South Seas islands. They would sketch and paint and live a simple life, wanting for nothing more than to be in each other's company forever.

Mischievously Meg had said the night before to a blushing Viola,

"We will send our children back to Glentorran for holidays so they understand their roots. And get to know